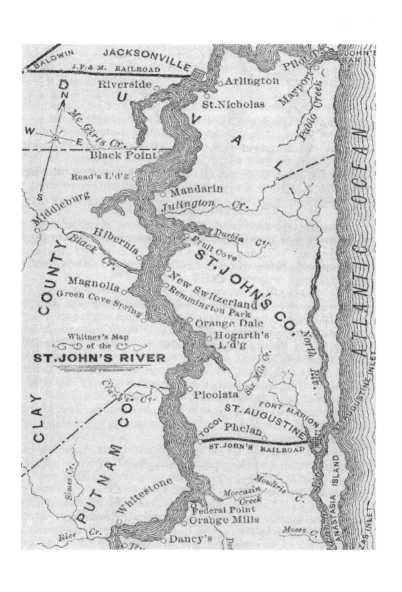

Cracker Landing
By
Louis E. Tagliaferri

Other Novels by the Author

This is a work of historical fiction. The names, characters, places, events and incidents portrayed in this novel either are the product of the author's imagination or are used fictionally. Any other resemblance to actual persons, living or dead, or actual events is purely coincidental.

Cover art is an image of a painting titled "The Hammock House" by Jackson Walker. Mr. Walker's courtesy in allowing an image of his work to be used for this purpose is greatly appreciated. Interior images are PD-Old and/or PD-Art.

Published by Louis E. Tagliaferri 2019

Ponte Vedra, Florida 32081

Contact: loutag38@gmail.com

Printed in the United States of America

Library of Congress

ISBN – 13: 9781796378252

Dedication

This book is dedicated to the memory of the thousands of pioneers, settlers and homesteaders whose courage, commitment and endurance helped shape the culture and land that is now the State of Florida.

Prologue

Doc CARTER CUT THE POWER on his new sixteen-foot Carolina Skiff, threw out the bumpers on the starboard side and let the boat glide up to the fish camp pier. With the bumpers cushioning the skiff, he leaned over and fastened the bowline to a cleat on the pier. Then he stepped onto the pier deck and tied a stern line to another cleat. Two other fishing boats were already tied up at the pier: a fifteen-foot Sun Tracker with a 60 HP Mercury and an old twenty-foot pontoon boat of uncertain make with a paint-peeled 25 HP Johnson. A few feet away from the pier, a black Ford Explorer trailering a bass boat slowly backed down the boat-launching ramp. Standing on the bow of the boat, a teenage boy shouted, "A little more to the left, dad." Doc Carter recognized the driver and the boy and went over to help.

"You got it right on, Zeke," he said to the driver of the Explorer. Then he helped the boy slip off the straps securing the boat while his father pulled the car and trailer up to the parking lot. Zeke's son, Tommy, started the boat's 40 HP Evinrude and skillfully backed it around to the pier where he tied it behind Doc Carter's boat.

"Thanks, Doc," Zeke said as he walked down the long wood deck that ran from the parking lot past the fish camp store and café to the pier. "Looks like you got yourself a nice new

1

skiff," he added gesturing to Doc Carter's new boat. "When did you pick that up?"

"It's barely a week old. Not really broken in yet," Doc Carter replied. "But, I like it fine. Past few days I've been targeting trout and flounder between the flood tides. What are you and Tommy going after today?"

"Reds," Zeke answered. "I've got black crab flies that the reds like a lot. We're going down river a bit to the shallows around the oyster flats. I told Annie to bake a loaf of cornbread because we're having reds for dinner! How about you? Catch anything worthwhile?"

Doc Carter held up a large white pail. "Look for yourself," he said. Inside were two, foot and a half long flounders thrashing around in river water.

"Damn! That'll do," Zeke said. "Well, we best be getting out there before somebody else gets those reds. By the way, Doc, I think it's time for Daisy's shots. Can I bring her over Monday?"

"That will be fine, Zeke. See you then." Doc Carter was a veterinarian who lived up river in Palm Valley. He was near retirement and was doing his best to cut back on his practice. Still, he found it difficult to turn down the folks he had known for many years and their beloved pets.

Helping Zeke and his son shove off from the pier, Doc Carter walked back to the fish camp café. It was time for a cool beer and maybe a basket of fried oysters and fries. He put the pail with the flounder in the back of his pickup and covered it with a tarp to shade it from the afternoon sun. Then he climbed the steps to the fish camp's covered porch, picked out a table and sat down. An attractive woman in her late thirties came over to the table carrying a condiment caddy and a set of silverware wrapped in a paper napkin. She smiled, placed the caddy and silverware on the table and sat down.

"Good afternoon, Doc. What'll it be today?"

"Howdy Jennie. What's your mom making today?"

"Just what you want, I suspect," Jennie replied with another smile. "Let's see. This is November. There is an "R" in the month meaning that..."

"Meaning that it's oyster season," Doc Carter laughed. "Yep. That and some fries and slaw," he said. "Oh, and please tell Bubba back there that I'd like a Corona Extra."

"Will do," Jennie said as she got up, walked past a handful of tables on the porch and entered the kitchen. She gave her mother Doc Carter's order and told her father that Doc wanted a Corona Extra. Jennie's father, Tim, acquired the moniker Bubba when his early patrons thought it funny that a Rhode Island Yankee would move down to Florida to open a Cracker fish camp. The title sort of made Tim an honorary Cracker. A couple of minutes later, Tim walked out onto the porch with two cold beers in his hands. He sat down at Doc Carter's table, popped the caps off the bottles and gave one beer to his guest. The two men clinked bottles, each then taking a swallow of the cool amber liquid. Placing his bottle on the table, Tim said, "You know, Doc, November in my opinion is the best time of the year down here."

"Are you glad that you and Beth moved here," Doc Carter said.

"Absolutely! Moreover, we're glad that Jennie also decided to come down here after her divorce. She's been a big help running this place."

"Jennie is an attractive young woman," Doc Carter observed. "I don't imagine she will be down here that long before some young man spots her and that will be that."

"We've been down here almost three years, now," Tim said. "Jennie came down a year after we opened for business.

3

She's dated a couple of young fella's she met at church. But, she seems to be in no hurry to tie the knot again with anyone."

"Sorry, I didn't mean to pry," Doc Carter said.

Tim just looked off at the peaceful scene down river and across at Pine Island. "I can see how this place appealed to them so much," he said.

"Appealed to who, Tim?"

"To Beth's ancestors – the folks who first settled here," Tim answered.

"I did not know that the fish camp was owned by anyone in Beth's family," Doc Carter said.

"Not the fish camp," Tim explained. "Before we converted this to a fish camp it was a homestead. Didn't I ever tell you the story about it?"

"You once mentioned that the camp has quite a history. However, you never said anything more about it."

Jennie interrupted their thoughts as she brought out a basket of fried oysters with fries and slaw for Doc Carter. "Are these local oysters, Jennie?" he asked.

"No, you don't want to eat the oysters in the Tolomato. The water in the Intracoastal is not as clean as it once was, with all of the boats and the houses that have been built around here. These are Apalachicola oysters, the best, plumpest oysters you can buy," Jennie stated.

"Honey," Tim said to his daughter. "Bring the Doc and me another Corona and some fried shrimp for me," he added. "I think we might be here for some time." Then he leaned over the table as Doc Carter dipped one of the oysters in cocktail sauce and raised it to his mouth. "Well, my friend, let me tell you the about the history of this fascinating and beautiful place."

Chapter One

EVEN IN THE SUBDUED LIGHT, the swamp was alive with blooming plants like white swamp lilies and purple wild irises. White and blue heron treaded through the shallow water skirting around jutting cypress knees as they searched for insects, plant roots and minnows. A brief tropical shower had passed just a few minutes earlier and now sunlight was once again trying to penetrate the dense canopy of bald cypress, swamp tupelo and black gum trees. It was late afternoon, so the swamp was quiet. The only sounds heard were the melodious notes of raindrops being shed from the trees overhead as they struck the swamp's shallow tannin waters. Dodging the raindrops, water striders glided silently along the surface of the water feeding on dead insects while multicolored dragonflies darted back and forth searching for their next meal.

In the stillness of the swamp, Spanish moss hung limply from dead tree branches like wisps of ghostly bridal veils. A green blanket of duckweed algae covered the water giving the false appearance of a solid surface. Without making even a ripple, two reptilian eyes and a snout broke the surface of the algae, also known as water meal, as a four-foot alligator took a few breaths of fresh air before resuming its underwater search for small fish and crustaceans.

Not all of the swamp was covered by water – at least not all of the time. Patches of dry or mostly dry hammocks were scattered throughout the wetland making habitats for small creatures like rats, mice, squirrels and even rabbits. The hammocks, that rose only a foot or so above the water level of the swamp, gave solid footing to the tall soft and hardwood trees covering much of the wetland. At the edge of one of the hammocks, next to a well-trod path made by foraging wild pigs, a swamp rat made its way hoping to find fallen berries and seeds. As it approached a mottled patch of leaves and pine straw, the rodent suddenly stopped and raised itself on its hind legs. Nervously, its eyes darted from side to side and its nose twitched as it searched for the danger it sensed.

Without warning, a five-foot diamondback rattlesnake that had been lying in wait under a palmetto bush, struck at a speed the eye could not follow and sank its venomous fangs into the hapless rodent. The diamondback held its prey tight in its jaws until the creature ceased struggling and then swallowed it whole. Coiling back to its hidden position, the snake waited patiently for its next victim. It did not have to wait for long. The silence of the swamp and hammock was broken by the voice of a child calling after her pet feral cat as the animal ran toward the swamp along the path made by the wild hogs. Abandoning all caution, the nine-year old girl ran after the cat, fearful of the dangers it would face if it entered the swamp.

"Stop Sissy! Sissy please stop!" the child cried. "Don't go in there," she screamed as the cat bounded along the wild hog path getting closer and closer to the mottled patch of leaves and pine straw next to the palmetto bush. In the distant background, a mother's voice could be heard shouting frantically, "Tammy! Tucker, she ran after the cat…in the swamp!"

The cat stopped just short from the palmetto bush. Although somewhat domesticated as the result of being adopted by Millie and Jessie Beckham's daughter, Tammy, the cat's feral survival instincts warned that it was in grave danger. Tammy caught up to the cat, reached down and picked it up. "Sissy, you naughty kitty..." Just then, no more than four feet away, the diamondback slithered out from under the palmetto bush, raised itself into striking position and began rattling its tail. Tammy and the cat froze in terror. At that moment, from behind Tammy, a loud shot rang out and the snake's head disappeared in a red mist.

Casually, Tammy's thirteen-year-old brother Tucker stepped forward from behind her. The young teen was carrying his father's Mississippi Rifle, its barrel still smoking, and calmly said, "Tammy, mama told you never to go into the swamp alone." He pointed to the headless body of the diamondback still withering on the ground. "That's why," he said. Then he picked up the snake's body and said, "You hold on to Sissy and I'll take this. Now, let's go home."

***

It was a hot, sultry Sunday evening in 1856, eleven years since Florida became the twenty-seventh state of the Union. Jessie Beckham, his wife Millie and Jessie's sister Ellen relaxed on the porch of their dogtrot farm house on a homestead the locals called "Cracker Landing." The landing was simply a wood pier jutting into the Tolomato River twelve miles north of St. Augustine, Florida. Jessie's father Adam built the pier so he could ship the turpentine he distilled from rosin, the raw gum, or dip from pine trees, and other products of his labor down river to St. Augustine where they could be sold at the market in Constitution Plaza.

Jessie Beckham was never sure why his father Adam decided to move his wife Stella and their young family to Florida from Georgia where the Beckham family had lived since emigrating from England in the late 1700s. Jessie knew that the

7

elder Beckham had worked on a plantation owned by a wealthy landowner named William Brailsford and his son-in-law James Troup. The plantation, called Broadfield, was located adjacent to the cypress swamps of the Altamaha River near Brunswick, Georgia. It was a very large indigo and rice plantation encompassing over 7,000 acres and employing 357 slaves. Adam Beckham was one of the plantation's fifteen white overseers.

Like the other overseers, Adam lived with his family on the plantation in one of the tabby houses provided by Brailsford and Troup. Adam's job was somewhat different from that of the other overseers. Most overseers 'bossed' the slaves who worked the fields planting, irrigating and harvesting indigo and rice. Adam 'bossed' a couple dozen slaves whose job was to maintain the plantation's extensive infrastructure, including the main plantation building called the Hofwyl House and all of the outbuildings. How Adam learned the carpenter skills required for that job was uncertain. However, Jessie, who was ten years old when his family moved to Florida, thought it had something to do with his father being a ships' carpenter in his youth. In any event, Adam apparently found the work tolerable and it paid better than the jobs of most overseers on the plantation.

Adam's wife Stella was the daughter of a local farmer who grew cotton, a cash crop that in most years provided enough income to support the family adequately. Adam met Stella at a church social event held during one of the years when excessive rain ruined much of the cotton crop in the area, including the crop on the farm of Stella's parents. Stella was sixteen at the time - the oldest of six children. One less child to support would definitely ease the financial burden brought about by a poor cotton crop. Therefore, Stella's parents were very receptive when Adam proposed to marry her.

Jessie was the youngest of Adam and Stella's four children – three boys and a daughter. Jessie's oldest brother, Benjamin, had enlisted in the St. Augustine militia when he was seventeen years old. Three years later, in 1835, he was one of over 100 soldiers killed in an Indian ambush called the Dade Massacre that occurred during the Second Seminole War. A couple of years later, Jessie's other brother, Samuel, decided to seek his fortune in the fertile farming country of Florida's Panhandle in the area north of Tallahassee. That left Jessie and his younger sister Ellen to help their parents farm the homestead and make a survivable living.

As with most Cracker families, Adam and Stella Beckham had raised their children to be as hard working as they were themselves. From the time the boys could hold a hammer or a hoe, Adam taught them all of the skills they would need to become self-sufficient farmers – and in this case also producers of rosin and turpentine. For his part, Jessie learned when and how to plant corn, peas, beans, squash, tomatoes and even sugar cane on the two acres that his father had set aside for agrarian purposes. He learned everything needed to raise, roundup and butcher the handful of scrub cows that roamed the open range near the Beckham homestead. He also learned how to tend to the horses and the mule they used to plow the fields and haul logs used for firewood or to make various wood products like tables, chairs and chests.

Jessie's father also taught him and his brothers how to load and shoot both muzzle-loaded long guns and single shot percussion pistols. These were invaluable "tools" for use when hunting wild hogs in the brush and swamp and for protection against critters like alligators and rattlesnakes, both of which were commonly found throughout the 150 acres of the Beckham homestead. Most of all, however, Adam Beckham taught his sons how to make turpentine.

Adam Beckham never considered himself much of a farmer. He farmed only out of necessity, as did most every Cracker in Florida. Most foodstuff needed by a Cracker family, especially fresh vegetables and meat, was grown on their own homestead. Flour, rice, salt, and some other dry goods, however, were only available in the markets downriver in St. Augustine. In order to have the money necessary to purchase those goods, Adam needed some source of revenue. He did this by tapping the pine trees on and around Cracker Landing and distilling the gum or dip to make turpentine and rosin. Then, he would take barrels of both marine products downriver on the sturdy flatboat he made or by hitching a ride on one of the keelboats that stopped at Cracker Landing on their way downriver from the lumber mill at the far northern end of the Tolomato River.

Whenever Adam made enough turpentine to take to market, he would simply fly a yellow pendant on a staff mounted on the pier to alert lumber mill keelboats to stop at Cracker Landing. Keelboat deckhands would signal their arrival by clanging an old ship's bell that Adam had mounted on the pier for that purpose. Occasionally, Adam would take Stella and one or more of the children with him for a day of supply shopping in St. Augustine. However, that was a long trip and often required an overnight's stay, sleeping on the open deck of the keelboat.

While Adam was teaching his sons the skills required for successful homesteading, his wife, Stella, taught her only daughter, Ellen, how to spin yarn, knit, sew, cook and tend to the chickens. She taught her how to make soap by boiling pig fat, water and lye made from wood ash over an open fire until the mixture thickened. She then added salt to solidify the mixture that was used to keep the house clean and free from crawling insects. She also taught the boys and Ellen to read, write and do arithmetic up to the third grade level, which was all they needed to function effectively in Cracker Florida in the mid-1800s. Stella made sure that they used their reading skills to study the bible. Also, to the extent there was any social life in the area, she maintained what contact was possible with other settler families.

That was many years ago. Tragically, both Adam and Stella died of yellow fever during the epidemic that scourged northern Florida in 1838 when they were visiting Samuel to help establish his homestead. That left only Jessie, age eighteen, and his sister Ellen, age seventeen, to run the Cracker Landing homestead. They rarely saw Samuel and Ellen never married. Together, Jessie and Ellen did their best to work Cracker Landing and, for the most part, they were successful. Jessie never acquired his father's carpentry skills. While he did the rough work needed to maintain the house and outbuildings, the part of the family income his father derived from making and selling wood products at the St. Augustine market was lost. Fortunately, Jessie was able to continue to produce and sell rosin and turpentine.

Making and selling turpentine was a profitable business. In order to make turpentine, only two things were needed: a lot of healthy pine trees and a turpentine still in good working order. The first requirement was easily fulfilled. Florida was covered with pine forests. As for the still, Jessie never learned how his father acquired the copper kettle and coils. However, he suspected that his father bartered it with merchants downriver in exchange for future barrels of turpentine. Once they were acquired, the turpentine making process was fairly simple, though sometimes dangerous.

All of the distilled substances except water were quite flammable and even explosive in vapor form. In one case, Adam allowed the mixture to boil too fast and the kettle exploded. Luckily, he had gone to fetch more firewood and was not injured in the explosion, which, not surprisingly, ruined the kettle. From that time on, Adam made sure that the fire under the kettle was not allowed to burn too fast or too hot.

Not long after Adam began distilling turpentine another use of distillation occurred to him. Adam grew a lot of corn. As he learned from other Crackers, corn mash could be fermented and distilled into a rather potent bush whiskey that the locals soon named Cracker Landing Lightning. Of course, part of the fermentation process required sugar, which is why Adam also grew a large crop of sugar cane. It also meant that Adam needed another still, easily obtained by bartering several barrels of turpentine for a used copper still with coils during one of Adam's trips to St. Augustine. However, cutting sugar cane, squeezing the juice from the cut canes, boiling the juice down until only raw sugar crystals were left, adding the sugar to the mash, letting it ferment until it frothed and then distilling it was a lot of work – more work than Adam and his son Jessie could handle.

Adam solved that problem by periodically inviting a few of the lumber mill men, who regularly stopped at Cracker Landing on their way downriver to St. Augustine, to help him cut and process the sugar cane crop. That enabled Adam to distill a goodly amount of Cracker Landing Lightning; a generous quantity of which he distributed to the men from the mill who helped him. He also made sure that a jug or so of good Cracker Landing bush whiskey was always available to the lumber mill's keelboat deck hands who dropped off the supplies he needed as they made their way back upriver to the mill. After Adam died, Jessie continued the practice, which ensured that the lumber mill keelboats made Cracker Landing a favorite stop between the mill and St. Augustine. In fact, that is how Jessie met his future wife Millie Sutter.

Chapter Two

IT WAS LATE MORNING in early October 1842. All of the summer crops had been harvested and it was not yet time to plant winter crops like squash, collard, turnips, mustard greens, cabbages and onions. Jessie was replacing the palm thatch roof of an open-air stall near the house used to give the horses and mule shelter from the sun. His sister Ellen was sitting on the front porch of the house stitching together pieces of a patchwork quilt she had been working on for over a month. The only sounds were made by the snorting of the horses and the rustle of palm leaves as Jessie wove them into the roof of the stall. Unexpectedly, they heard the clanging of the bell down by the pier signaling the arrival of the sawmill barge. Both of them put their tasks aside and walked down the path leading to the landing.

"Looks like we have company," Jessie said to Ellen as he spotted a couple of deckhands he knew walking toward them. The men were accompanied by an attractive young woman in her late teens. Ellen was delighted when she saw the young woman, who seemed to be close to her own age. Female visitors to Cracker Landing were a rarity. She looked forward to chatting with her.

"Hey there Jessie," the taller of the two men shouted as the three visitors approached the two Beckhams.

"Amos, you scoundrel!" Jessie responded jokingly. "And who is that malcontent with you? Oh, it's you Toby," he said laughing as he greeted Amos's assistant. "What brings you to Cracker Landing today? I don't have any turpentine to send to the market yet."

Amos Peabody snorted and pointed to a lanky, bearded man about forty years old who stepped off the pier and began walking toward the group. "That there is Tom Sutter, the new sawmill foreman and this here is Tom's daughter Millie."

"Well, a pleasure to meet you, Miss Sutter," Jessie said. "This is my sister, Ellen."

The two women smiled at each other and Millie said, "I'm just Millie – not Miss Sutter."

"And I'm Tom," her father said as he joined the group.

The men shook hands and then Amos said, "Tom and Millie and Tom's wife Sarah just came down here from Savannah where Tom was a logging boss for a mill up there. The reason we stopped is that Millie was curious to know what a Florida Cracker is and I figured that if anybody knew it's you, Jessie!"

Everyone laughed and Jessie said, "I knew you were a scoundrel, Amos. What have you been telling these folks?"

"Well, for one thing, I've been telling them about Cracker Landing Lightning, the best bush whiskey in these parts."

"I knew you had a motive," Jessie said. "Come on up to the house. Let's get out of the sun and I'll see if I can round up a drop or two of Lightning."

Jessie found an open jug of Lightning and took the men to the stall he was working on where they sat in the shade and talked about rumors that the federal government was thinking about granting Florida and Iowa statehood, rather than continue their status as territories. They also talked about the abolition movement up north and how badly it would affect plantation owners if slavery were abolished. Meanwhile, Ellen and Millie sat on the porch refreshing themselves with cool water drawn from the homestead well as Millie admired the patchwork quilt Ellen was making. During their conversation, Millie said she heard that the term Cracker came from the sound a cow hunter's whip made when he cracked it to herd the open range cows or to scare off alligators. Ellen laughed. "There are only a few cowboys up here in these parts. So, instead, we say that we got that name from cracking dried corn to make mash for whiskey!" Both of the women roared with laughter.

As time passed, Ellen and Millie became close friends and Millie became a frequent visitor to Cracker Landing. At each visit, Jessie noticed how beautiful Millie was. He loved her warm, open personality and her frequent lighthearted, jaunty laughter. In turn, Millie admired Jessie for his upbeat attitude, gentleness and for his strong character. It was not too long before this mutual admiration turned to love and one day Jessie asked Millie's for her hand in marriage.

Ellen was ecstatic to learn that Jessie and Millie planned to marry. While somewhat sad that she, herself, had not found anyone special, Ellen looked forward to the female companionship Millie's presence would bring to Cracker Landing. She and Millie worked with Millie's mother Sarah to plan a simple yet fun wedding. The biggest problem was finding a preacher to marry the couple. The Sutter and Beckham families had been members of the Church of England, as were many descendants of English immigrants to Colonial America. The nearest – actually, the only – church of that faith was Trinity Parish, an Episcopal Church founded in St. Augustine in 1830. It was not practicable to transport a wedding party downriver to St. Augustine, and the Sutter farm was quite difficult to reach.

Therefore, it was decided to hold the wedding at Cracker Landing and bring the guests and preacher there by keelboat.

Fortunately, the then rector of Trinity Parish, Rev. R.A. Henderson, was more than willing to oblige. He and his predecessors were doing what they could to establish an Episcopal diocese in the St. Augustine area – a difficult task in a predominantly Catholic city. The idea of expanding his flock, even at a distance, was very appealing to him. As a result, on June 22, 1843, Jessie Beckham and Millie Sutter stood on the porch of the Cracker Landing home before Rev. Henderson and were pronounced man and wife. Witnessing the brief ceremony were the bride's parents, Tom and Sarah Sutter, and several keelboat deckhands including Amos and Toby. Everyone had a great time. There was food and plenty of Cracker Landing Lightning for all and there was even music and dancing, thanks to Amos who played a "mean" fiddle. That night, Ellen discretely accepted Mrs. Henderson's invitation to join her and the Reverend on the return keelboat trip to St. Augustine where she would spend the night with them.

Tucker Beckham was born in 1844. Two year later, Millie had a miscarriage in her fourth month. For some while it seemed that Tucker would be an only child. However, the sadness of her miscarriage and fear that she might not be able to carry a child again was overcome when Tammy Beckham was born in 1849. Aunt Ellen was loved dearly by the children and was a great aid in raising them. Just as his parents had done, Jessie ensured that his son learned everything that he could teach him about running and maintaining the homestead – including making turpentine and, yes, making good Cracker Landing Lightning.

Jessie also taught Tucker how to load and shoot the family rifle, a newer model 1841 Mississippi Percussion Rifle manufactured by the Harpers Ferry Armory in West Virginia and an 1845 Colt single Action Revolver. Jessie often took

Tucker hunting with him. The area was filled with deer, wild turkey and wild hogs – the latter tracing their heritage to the first Spanish Period in Florida. The Spanish Conquistadores introduced pigs to the New World and let them loose to forage in the open range and swamps where they proliferated.

There were many other wild creatures near the family homestead, some of them very dangerous. Among the more common dangerous species native to the area were alligators and Diamondback rattlesnakes, like the one that threatened Tammy and her cat Sissy. Luckily for his sister and her cat, by the time he was thirteen years old, Tucker had become an excellent shot.

As Tucker grew older, he became increasingly curious about the family history. He knew very little about his paternal grandparents or, for that matter, about his uncles, Benjamin and Samuel. He was aware that Benjamin had joined the Army and that he was killed fighting Seminole Indians. He also knew that Samuel had moved to the north central part of Florida to stake out his own homestead and that his paternal grandparents, Adam and Stella, both died from yellow fever while visiting him there. One day while helping his father tap pine trees for sap, Tucker pressed his father for more information about the family's past.

"You sure are a curious one," Jessie said. "The truth is that your grandpaw never much wanted to talk about his past. However, when a family lives together in a small house, the children are bound to overhear their parents talk about things."

Jessie paused to pour a tin cup of pine dip into a bucket and refasten the cup to one of the trees. Then he continued. "I believe that your grandpaw and nanna ran into some kind of trouble when they lived in Georgia and had to leave in a hurry. However, they were very careful not to talk about it when they thought we kids could hear them. The truth is that I do not know the full story. Benjamin and Samuel likely knew more about why they left that I did – they were older than me. But, now that you have become a responsible young man, I will tell you what I know. There is one thing that I can tell you right at the start. It seems to me that my paw, your grandpaw, stumbled upon a pot full of trouble that he wished he had never found."

Chapter Three

ADAM BECKHAM KNEW HE had to leave the Broadfield Plantation soon – now actually. When he told his wife Stella what happened and that he had decided they must move, she simply said she understood and agreed. They also agreed to never discuss their reason for leaving with their two young sons. Practically everything Adam and his family used at Broadfield was owned and supplied by the plantation owners: the house they lived in, its furnishings, tools and even the few livestock they kept for personal use. They had very little to bring with them to their new home – wherever that might be. Adam had a small amount of money he carefully saved over the years. That was the stake he would need to start life over again; hopefully a better life than they were leaving.

The location choices they confronted were straightforward. A deep southern family like the Beckhams would have little acceptance in the northern abolition states. Besides, the thought of having to deal with the harsh climate of northern areas, even the Carolina Mountains to the west, was not appealing to them. In the end, there were only two practicable alternatives. They could follow the route of many Carolina and Georgia settlers who moved to the fertile, rolling land above Tallahassee in the newly designated Territory of Florida or, alternatively, relocate to the territory's northeast coastal region. Adam chose the latter because he learned that the land north of St. Augustine was very similar to that around Broadfield Plantation: broad estuaries and marshes, extensive pine forests, open plains in which livestock could forage, some fertile ground for farming and, freshwater swamps, which were always a good source of food for skilled hunters. The only remaining question was how to get there.

At the time Spain ceded Florida to the United States, the road system along the coast in both Georgia and the northeast part of the Territory of Florida was rudimentary at best. The journey south from the Broadfield Plantation to St. Augustine would have been long and tortuous, spanning about 125 miles and ten-days travel by horse and wagon. Fortunately, by 1822, Brunswick, Georgia, only a few miles south of the Broadfield Plantation, was becoming an important Atlantic Coast port. Therefore, the Beckhams decided that the most practical way to reach St. Augustine was by ship.

It took Adam, Stella and the boys less than a day to reach Brunswick where Adam sold the horse and pack mule that carried all of their personal possessions. At the customs house, located next to the marine piers, Adam paid a fare of $1.75 each for him and Stella - no fare was required for the boys. The family then boarded the sailing ship Conasauga, a 450-ton barque that departed from Brunswick at high tide on Sunday, July 21, 1822. The seas were mostly calm, which was fortunate since this was the first time that the Beckhams had been to sea. One hundred six miles and twenty-one hours later, they arrived outside of the entrance to St. Augustine Harbor, where they had to wait five hours for another high tide so the Conasauga could cross over the shallow St. Augustine bar and enter the harbor.

In the early 1800s, St. Augustine became the seat of St. Johns County, a large region that stretched from the Atlantic Ocean west to the Apalachee River. Even though St. Augustine was the most important city in all of northeast Florida, its population was less than 3,000. The territorial government formed by Andrew Jackson, who was appointed military governor by President Monroe in 1821, was determined to increase the city and county's population by attracting settlers to the territory. In order to accomplish this, Governor Jackson established a program of incentives to replace the former system of Spanish Land Grants. Under the new system, public lands, which at the time included almost all of Florida's interior, were awarded to settlers at little or no cost if they worked the land and remained on it as their domicile for five years.

When he arrived in St. Augustine, Adam Beckham made his way as quickly as possible to the county land grant office. He learned that considerable acreage was available right in the county north of St. Augustine up to the St. Johns River. The problem was that Adam had no knowledge whatsoever regarding what parcels within that area were good prospective homesteading lands – until he met Jacob Mickler, who had immigrated to Florida while it was still under Spanish rule. Mickler and his wife, Manuela, owned a homestead about twenty-five miles north of St. Augustine in an area the Spanish had called Diego Plains. A broad 60,000-acre tract of timber and grazing land, the plains derived its name from its first owner, Don Diego Espinoza, who acquired it under a land grant from the Spanish Crown in 1703.

Mickler told Adam that there was a good tract of land about twelve miles north of St. Augustine on the west side of the Tolomato River opposite a small pine-covered island the Spanish named Isla de Piños, Pine Island.

"I tell you, Adam, from what you seem to want, that's the perfect tract of land," Mickler said. "It's right on the Tolomato River no more than six hours from here, depending on the tide."

21

"That's important, Jacob," Adam agreed. "I would need some practical way to get my farm products to the market here in St. Augustine and, at the same time, bring supplies from here up to the homestead."

"That tract has a lot of pine trees and pine trees mean turpentine," Mickler opined. "Turpentine and rosin. There is even a better market here for rosin than turpentine."

"Why is that?" Adam inquired.

"Well sir, one reason is that the boat yards here use rosin for caulking the ships' seams," Mickler explained.

Mickler also told Adam that the tract bordered the Diego Swamp, which was at the bottom of Diego Plains. Excellent wild hog and deer hunting there, he said. "By the way," Mickler said. "I am heading back up to my farm day after tomorrow. You are welcome to come with me. I will be more than happy to help you set up a temporary camp so you can begin clearing your land for a house.

"I would appreciate that," Adam said. "However, I have no way to pay you for your kindness."

Mickler chuckled, "That's not how it works here, Adam. Neighbors help neighbors and nobody expects to be paid for helping. I am sure that in the future I will need help for something and you can repay me the favor then."

Adam thanked Mickler, then immediately went to the land office and applied for a grant for that tract. Tracts of land farther inland were being made available free of charge in order to induce settlers to move west. However, there was a price on the tract Adam wanted – seventy-five cents per acre. Relieved at learning the low cost, Adam requested a tract of 125 acres, including Pine Island. Upon payment of $100.00, including a stamp fee, Adam and Stella became the owners of a property they had not yet even seen – the Beckham homestead.

Stella Beckham was delighted when Adam told her about the homestead purchase. Since arriving in St. Augustine a couple of days earlier, the Beckhams had found temporary refuge at the home of Reverend and Mrs. M. J. Mott on St. Francis Street. Reverend Mott was the second rector of the newly created Episcopal parish in St. Augustine. Still without a church building, Reverend Mott conducted Sunday services in the old Government Building that had been used as the Spanish Headquarters when they controlled the territory. Mrs. Mott told Stella that she and the boys could stay with her and the Reverend until Adam was able to set up a place for them to live on their new homestead.

Three days later, a forty-foot keelboat en route to the sawmill located at the head of the Tolomato River stopped at a shell midden on the west bank of the river. Adam thought it was the most beautiful, peaceful place he had ever seen. Dozens of white heron, ibis and egrets lined the shore of Pine Island, across the river from where the keelboat had landed, as though waiting to welcome the newcomers. Brown and black anhinga, also called snakebirds, broke the surface of the river clutching a catch of fish in their beaks. On the west shore, several blue heron took to the air flying side-by-side with wood storks. High overhead, red-tailed hawks screeched incessantly to each other signaling that they had found some hapless squirrel or rodent in the field below.

On the shore, palmetto bushes were everywhere and rising tall among them were stout sable palms, their fan-like leaves shading the ground below. Looking west, Adam could see a broad, flat backshore area leading toward a thick forest of southern pine trees. However, toward the north there seemed to be the beginning of a freshwater swamp with thirty-foot magnolias guarding a dense forest of bald cypress. He could also see swamp tupelos and live oak with ghostly wisps of

Spanish moss, hanging languidly from their upstretched branches.

Adam, Jacob Mickler and three of the keelboat deck hands unloaded Adam's supplies and tools from the boat and stacked them on a dry shell midden. Next, they struggled to persuade an old mule named Sally that Adam bought from the livery stable to disembark by walking down a narrow plank that led from the deck to the shell-strewn shore. Sally balked, but eventually the stubborn critter was led off the boat. When everything Adam acquired in St. Augustine was unloaded, he, Jacob and the keelboat crew began looking for a site on which to build a temporary shelter. About fifty yards inland from the river, they found a raised, flat area that seemed to be ideal. Several hours later, the ground around the site had been cleared of brush and a raised platform with a palm branch covered roof had been erected.

"That's all we can do for now," Mickler said to Adam. "You should be fine here. That type of platform was called a 'chickee' by the Indians who lived here long ago. Actually, it is still used by the Indians who live west of here in the Ocala area."

"The chickee is high enough so you won't be bothered by any of the critters that might roam around here during the night," one of the keelboat deckhands opined. "Lots of wild hogs in those woods over there. Damn mean critters. Snakes and gators, too."

"That's right," Mickler agreed. "However, most likely the only things you will need to worry about are the mosquitos. They will start coming out at dusk. You will be wise to keep a smoky fire burning all night to keep them from bothering you too much."

Mickler pointed to the keelboat crew and added, "The men here will stop by on their next trip downriver in a day or so to see how you are doing. In the meanwhile, we had better be

24

moving on. I want to be home before dark and we still have another hour or so left to reach the sawmill. I live a half-hour west of there."

Adam thanked Jacob and the keelboat crew once more and accompanied them to the river where they had anchored the keelboat. As the crew raised anchor, one of the deckhands hollered out to Adam, "If you want us to stop here regularly, you'll need to build a pier out into the river. This is a tidal river and when the tide is going out, we won't be able to get anywhere near the shore."

Adam shouted that he would make a pier a priority project and waved to crew as they rowed and sculled the keelboat upriver.

Cracker Landing

26

Chapter Four

FOR THE NEXT WEEK, Adam spent his time clearing out brush and small trees in the area where he planned to build a cabin. He also cut down several pine trees adjacent to the site and then cut them again into lengths the size needed for cabin walls. It was ceaseless work from the time the sun rose in the morning until dusk. He had to stop then because he was exhausted and because it was too dark to work safely. He also explored the area immediately surrounding his homestead, locating a freshwater spring not far from the site and venturing into the swamp where he shot some game to supplement his diet of beans, peas and hard tack washed down by black and very bitter coffee. After he built a smoke rack, he was able to cure the game he shot the fish he caught in the river. Soon, his diet was filled with a variety of smoked meat and fish such as wild turkey, venison, mullet, trout and red fish. He missed Stella and the boys. However, there was more work to do before he could fetch them from St. Augustine.

One night, the mosquitos were especially bad. There was not a breath of air stirring and a recent rain shower seemed to have brought the voracious insects out in record numbers. In addition to keeping a smoking fire up wind of the chickee at night, Adam spread crushed French Mulberry and Wax Myrtle leaves around his bedroll on the chickee platform. That combination, plus the fact that he slept fully clothed, usually kept the mosquitos at bay. This night was different, however and the insects were especially bothersome. Adam got up in the middle of the night to put more branches on the fire. Actually, he found that burning punk wood, the decaying center of a tree or log, gave off an odor that was very effective in repelling mosquitos.

Adam threw more punk wood on the fire and turned back toward the ladder leading up to the platform. On the ground between him and the ladder, less than ten feet away, stood the most ornery wild hog he had ever seen. The creature was a sow that must have weighed two or three hundred pounds. It sported both an upper and lower set of very sharp tusks. Tusks were normally used for defense by female hogs and for fighting other boars by male hogs. The hog confronting Adam was accompanied by two piglets. All three had apparently been rooting near the chickee for roots, insects, tubers and acorns. They were likely attracted to the light of the fire when, unfortunately, they stationed themselves between the fire and chickee ladder, thereby trapping Adam.

Adam had nothing with which to defend himself. His rifle and even his long knife were up on the platform. Not even a shovel was within reach. Meanwhile, it seemed that the temporary standoff was soon to come to a climax as Adam saw the sow paw the ground, snort and become increasingly nervous as her piglets wandered closer to where Adam was standing. Adam knew that without a weapon, he was at a definite disadvantage if the sow charged. He slowly took the only route open to him. He backed inch-by-inch toward the fire until he was almost on top of it. Just then, a piglet dashed between him and the sow and that was all that was necessary to set the hog in motion. The sow charged to protect its piglet. At the same time, Adam reached into the fire and brought out a flaming branch, thrusting it right at the sow. The sow squealed, came to an abrupt stop and took off for the nearby woods with the piglets following as fast as they could. Adam vowed never again to leave the safety of the platform without either his revolver or rifle – or both!

It was not long before Adam returned to St. Augustine to collect Stella and the boys. The homestead site was still quite primitive when Stella first saw it. Adam was worried that she might be disappointed. After all, it was quite different from the plantation with the tabby overseer's house they had left behind. However, Stella saw the same beauty that Adam did when he first saw the site. She embraced him and then did what any pioneer wife and mother would do. She began to tidy things up in order to make the site more habitable for her husband and children. Then she made supper for all of them.

Thanks to Adam's diligence and hard work, almost all of the material needed to construct a cabin for the Beckham family was ready when Jacob Mickler, his wife and a team of men from the sawmill arrived one Sunday to help their new neighbor. Using the same carpenter skills that he employed at the Broadfield Plantation, Adam had already cut the timber to proper size and staked out the raised foundation of the cabin.

Adam opted for a single pen cabin that could be expanded to a dogtrot double pen in the future. A single pen cabin was one single room built on sturdy timbers that rested on either tabby or wood pillars about two feet above ground level. In this case, Adam chose to begin with a left pen, meaning that the mudbrick chimney was built on the left outside wall with a single entrance door on the wall opposite the chimney. The front and rear walls would have two windows each. As with most cabins build in Florida, there was no loft or attic because of the extreme summer heat.

For materials, Adam selected hardwood cypress for the supporting foundation pillars, longleaf pine logs for the cabin's walls and pine planks for the floor. Both woods were relatively resistant to termites and other insects, as well as rot resistant. The roof, at least temporarily, would be made of wattle thickly covered with palm leaves, which actually was a better insulator from the sun's searing heat than wood shingles. In addition to providing protection from insects and worse, the crawl space under the cabin allowed air to circulate and help cool the cabin interior. An exterior wraparound covered porch gave further respite from the sun and heat. Inside the cabin, the floor planks were spaced slightly apart to facilitate sweeping dirt from the floor and to allow better air circulation.

Throughout the day, Stella and Jacob's wife Manuela provide coffee, cool water and food for the men. Manuela also helped Stella keep the boys under control and out of the way of the men. By the end of the day, the cabin was fully erected. The furniture was yet to be built, but Adam planned to begin that in the morning. A jug of whiskey brought by one of the keelboat captain was passed around to celebrate the event and was even sampled by the two women. Then, much in debt to the kindness of their neighbors, Adam, Stella and the boys were alone. That night they slept inside their new cabin, bedrolls spread out on the floor.

Over the next few years, the simple Cracker cabin became a home and the homestead became a viable farm. Adam used his carpentry skills to build all of the furniture and woodwork needed in the cabin: beds, tables, chairs, cabinets and counters. Aided by his sons, Benjamin and Samuel, Adam built a pier extending into the Tolomato River that became known as Cracker Landing. He also purchased two copper stills; one for distilling turpentine from pinesap and the other for making a potent corn liquor the locals called Cracker Landing Lightning. Meanwhile, Stella was busy making blankets, quilts, pillows and clothes for her family that included two more children over the passing years, Jessie and Ellen. Then one spring day, a man walked up to the cabin from the landing - a Negro. He spotted Stella washing clothes on the front porch of the cabin and said, "Afternoon, Ma'am. Member me? I be Billie Jack."

Stella recognized Billie Jack the minute she saw him walking up the path from the landing. He was a tall, thin man with a white speckled beard that contrasted sharply with his dark, weathered skin. It had been several years since she last saw him at the Broadfield Plantation. He was stooped over now and walked with a limp, favoring his left leg. She thought he must be at least forty years old by now.

"Oh my dear Lord!" Stella exclaimed. "Billie Jack, is that really you?"

"Yez'um. It be me for real," Billie Jack replied.

"You look tired, Billie Jack. Come on up here out of the sun and have some of that cool water in the bucket," Stella said. Then she told five-year old Jessie, who was gawking at the black man stepping up onto the porch, to run and get his daddy. Adam and the two older boys, Benjamin and Samuel were out in the field tilling rows of rich soil where they planned to plant yellow corn. Jessie ran as fast as he could shouting "paw," all the way to the cornfield.

Adam left the two older boys to continue tilling the field while he made his way back to the cabin with Jessie in tow. He stopped and stared in disbelief when he saw Billie Jack sitting on the porch with Stella. Then he joined Stella and their unexpected visitor as a flood of memories and more than a little apprehension overcame him. Cautiously, Adam smiled at Billie Jack and said, "It's been a long time. How are you?"

Even though it had now been several years since Adam left Broadfield Plantation with Stella and the children, he had always harbored a feeling that the past would someday catch up with him. Billie Jack's arrival at their homestead seemed to be

31

proof of that. However, there was an earlier instance in St. Augustine that had also confirmed Adam's concern. One one occasion, Adam went to St. Augustine with the keelboat crew and a load of turpentine and rosin barrels because he wanted to speak with the customers about payments and prices. He had finished speaking with a buyer who represented a boatyard on the San Sabastian River when a man came up to him and said, "Excuse me, sir, but don't I know you?"

The man was from Brunswick, Georgia and said he recalled Adam coming into his blacksmith shop to buy a set of chisels and hammers. Adam tried to side step the assertion but the man, who introduced himself as Peter Bisbee, persisted.

"Ah, of course," Bisbee said. "You were the woodworking overseer at the Broadfield Plantation."

"Yes," Adam responded, he did work there.

"Well then," Bisbee continued, "You must remember that old bastard Karl Hofmann. If I recall correctly, he was one of the indigo planter's overseers."

"Yes, I remember him," Adam said uncomfortably.

"He was one of the most miserable people I ever met," Bisbee commented. "It's said he treated the slaves in a most unkind way. Beat them frequently for no good cause," he added. "A truly terrible person."

"That and then some," Adam stated.

"He is still there, I suppose," Bisbee said.

"No, actually, he is dead," Adam said and then immediately regretted the comment.

"You don't say. What happened?" Bisbee asked.

"I'm not sure. Some kind of accident, I believe," Adam replied. Then, Adam said he had many things to take care of in town and politely excused excuse himself.

"Where do you live, now?" Bisbee inquired, hastily.

"Quite far from here, actually. Now, I really must go. It was a pleasure meeting you again, Mr. Bisbee."

The incident was disconcerting to Adam. He hardly expected anyone from near Broadfield Plantation to be walking the streets of St. Augustine – particularly on one of the few days he was in town. However, it was the unexpected appearance of Billie Jack that bothered him the most. He had nothing to fear from Billie Jack, himself. In fact, just the opposite. It was Billie Jack who was in his debt. However, what concerned Adam more than anything were the memories that Billie Jack's reappearance brought to the surface. Memories he thought he had left behind years earlier.

Chapter Five

"WHERE ARE TUCKER AND TAMMY?" Jessie asked Millie. "It will be dusk soon and I don't want either of them, especially Tammy, roaming too far from the cabin."

"Tammy is in the cabin reading a book by Philip J. Cozans titled *Little Eva: Flower of the South*," Millie answered. The closest school for the children was twelve miles downriver at St. Augustine, a distance much too far for regular travel. Therefore, both Tammy and Tucker were home-schooled, as were most other Cracker children. Both Millie and Ellen served as the children's teachers. Millie had a seventh grade education and Ellen had finished the sixth grade. Together, the two women had all of the qualifications they needed to ensure that Tammy and Tucker would acquire the knowledge and skills required to be responsible, fully functioning citizens in the Cracker society of the mid-1800s.

"I believe Tucker is over by the smoke rack," Ellen said. "The last I saw him, he was drying the skin of that big Diamondback he shot when Millie sent him to fetch Tammy from the swamp."

"We have to watch that girl," Jessie observed. "She is getting a bit too bold for her own good."

"Well, I think almost getting bit by that rattler sobered her up this time," Millie opined. "At least I pray it did!"

The three adult Beckhams sat in silence for a while, watching the sun begin to set in the west. "What are you thinking about, Jessie?" Millie wondered. "You are awfully quiet."

"Oh, I was just thinking about some of the repairs Tucker and I have to make to the cabin. Both of the chimneys are getting old. The mud brick does not last forever and will soon need to be replaced," Jessie said, referring to the mud and stick construction of the chimneys.

"The chimney on your side of the cabin looks like it's ready to fall over," Ellen added.

"Both chimneys lean out," Jessie said. "That way, if the wood around them catches fire the chimneys could easily be pulled away from the cabin. However, I was also thinking about the time paw built your side of the cabin, Ellen."

The original Beckham cabin built by Jessie's father Adam and Jessie's older brothers Benjamin and Samuel was known as a single pen cabin with one large room. However, when Jessie's mother learned she was pregnant with Jessie, she told Adam that they really needed another room in the cabin. That second room, separated from the other by a covered walk through space called a dogtrot, eventually became the bedroom for the children, giving Adam and Stella much needed privacy. Later, it became the bedroom for Ellen, Tammy and Tucker. Of course, the original single pen also served as kitchen, dining area and family gathering room, although most cooking was done away from the house.

"That was the same time he built the pier," Ellen recalled.

"Yep, I guess with all the help he had then he felt it was a good time to get that work done."

"What help did he have?" Millie asked. "Do you mean you and your brothers?"

"He had their help for sure," Jessie said. "I was only about five years old at the time and Ellen was even younger. So, I was no real help and mama had her hands full. Part of the help I meant was the Negro man they called Billie Jack."

"Billie Jack," Ellen said thoughtfully. "I really do not recall the name."

"You wouldn't," Jessie said. "You were just a baby. I barely remember him. He was here for only a few weeks and then he was gone. Neither mama nor paw ever talked about him after that. But, I guess he helped paw a lot while he was here. I have no idea why, though."

***

The indigo storage barn on the Broadfield Plantation had been on Adam Beckham's repair list for a few weeks. The barn was little more than a large shed. Twenty-foot pine logs supported a slat roof covered with palm branches while rough-cut planks served as siding. Inside the fifty-foot by forty-foot structure, a two tiered rack system was installed in a U-shape along three sides. Outward opening barn doors completed the fourth side. After indigo was harvested and processed, it was dried to form a cake that was then cut into very hard, but light, one and one-half inch squares called 'pigeon necks' that were a sparkling, iridescent blue. The pigeon necks were stored in barrels until shipped to dyers. On the Broadfield Plantation, those barrels were stored in the indigo shed, some on the floor and others sitting on the second tier racks.

James Troup, son-in-law of the plantation owner Williams Brailsford, had instructed Adam to make needed repairs to the poles supporting the second tier racks in the indigo barn. At his last inspection of the barn, Troup noted that several of the supporting poles seemed to be in a precarious condition. Adam rounded up one of his carpenters, a tall, gaunt Negro named Billie Jack, and headed to the barn to make the repairs. As they approached the barn, they heard a scream and the sound of a struggle coming from inside. Forcing the closed barn door open, Adam and Billie Jack rushed in to see Karl Hofmann, the indigo overseer, whipping a young Negro slave named Harriet with his belt. The top of the woman's blouse had been torn and her right breast was exposed. She was huddled on the dirt floor of the barn begging him not to rape her, which was obviously his intent.

As Adam and Billie Jack rushed in, Hofmann turned toward them, flipping his belt to show the heavy buckle end. He then grabbed the young woman by the hair.

"This is none of your business, Beckham. Get out of here and take your bastard 'swap dog' with you!" Hofmann shouted, using a pejorative that referred to a slave who had been raised by non-relatives when his or her parents were sold to another slave owner.

Harriet was now crying hysterically. Billie Jack ran to her aid but Hofmann swung the buckle end of his belt at him striking Billie Jack on the head. Blood spurted from the wound. Adam took advantage of Hofmann's momentary distraction and charged at him, knocking the overseer to the ground. The two men rolled over on the floor each pounding the other with their fists. Then Hofmann broke free, reached behind his back and pulled out a long knife with a serrated blade from a sheath. He was ready to thrust it into Adam, who was scrambling to get up, when Billie Jack struck him in the back of the head with a hammer he picked up from Adam's toolbox. Hofmann staggered for an instant, dropped the knife and fell to the floor stone dead. Harriet fainted. Adam and Billie Jack stood, eyes wide open, gaping at the dead man on the floor.

"Oh my God!" Adam said in disbelief.

"Oh sweet Jesus!" Billie Jack cried out as he let the hammer drop from his hands.

Billie Jack revived Harriett, who was curled in a ball, whimpering. There was a moment of panic as the three of them realized the danger they were facing. The two slaves would surely be quickly tried and executed. Slaves who even struck their masters were brutally punished and death was certain if a slave killed any white person for any reason. Adam was in grave danger, too. At the very least, he would be seen as complicit in Hofmann's death. He would surely face imprisonment, if not execution, himself. However, he realized there was a possible way out. It would have to be that a terrible accident occurred.

Adam looked around the barn and noted that the incident happened immediately next to a barrel rack that was in poor condition. Several heavy barrels of 'pigeon neck' were positioned on the above rack. Adam told Billie Jack to help him drag Hofmann's body so that it was face down on the floor, directly under the barrels stacked on the rack. Then Adam spotted a discarded piece of rough-cut four-foot post. The heavy post was just what he needed. Ordering Billie Jack and Harriet to step away, Adam swung the post at one of the poles supporting the rack until the pole cracked and the rack of barrels tumbled down on top of Hofmann's body. Harriet screamed and fainted into Billie Jack's arms.

It was a gruesome sight. Barrels split, indigo pigeon neck cubes and indigo dust covered the floor, including Hofmann's crushed body. It was clear that any sign of the actual cause of his death was obliterated. Luckily, the barn was far enough away from the main house and other structures that all of this went unnoticed. Adam, Billie Jack and Harriet took an oath of secrecy and each one memorized the same story. Harriet was passing by the barn on her way back to the slave quarters from the indigo fields. Adam and Billie Jack were going to the barn to make repairs. They all heard a rumble coming from the barn and ran to see what happened. They saw that one of the racks had collapsed and then saw the body of Overseer Hofmann underneath. Despite their efforts, they were not able to pull the heavy material off Hofmann and quickly went to summon help.

There was an inquiry, of course. However, it was found that Billie Jack's head injury, Adam's bruised hand and face and Harriet's torn blouse were caused when they tried to free Hofmann from the fallen material. Fortunately, because Hofmann was intensely disliked, anyway, there was no interest on the part of the sheriff or the plantation owners to pursue the matter further. Still, life going forward would never be the same for Adam, Billie Jack or Harriet and there would always be a cloud of uncertainty hanging over the three of them. Adam decided that it would be unwise to remain at Broadfield Plantation.

Not long after Hofmann's death, Harriet was sold to a plantation owner in Savannah. She was never heard from again. The promise of free or low cost land grants to settlers willing to move to the new Territory of Florida was the just the incentive Adam needed to leave Broadfield. Several months after Adam and his family left the plantation, Billie Jack ran away. That was the last anyone heard about him, until that day he showed up at Cracker Landing.

Chapter Six

Ever SINCE JESSIE BECKHAM learned about the Bradley massacre in Pasco County near Tampa, he kept several loaded rifles and revolvers readily available in his Cracker Landing cabin. He also made sure that everyone living at the homestead knew how to load, aim and shoot all of the weapons. The story about the Bradley massacre terrified both Millie and Ellen. Tucker, however, seemed to take it in stride, while Tammy seemingly paid little attention to it.

According to the story, it was dusk on May 14, 1856. That evening, all seemed normal at the farm of Captain Robert Duke Bradley, Regular Army, a well-known pioneer and Indian fighter who was recovering from a serious health condition. Then, according to an article in the Palatka Democrat, May 22, 1856:

"Bradley's family had returned from supper, and the children were in an open passage of the house, when Indians fired a volley which killed a little girl and mortally wounded a boy fifteen years old; he ran into the house, got a gun and returned to the passage to return the fire when he fell dead. The mother, Mrs. Bradley, ran out and carried her children into the house. The Indians shot at her without hurting her or any more of the children. Capt. Bradley, who was prostrated on his bed with sickness, arose and

41

*returned a fire on the Indians with two or three guns which he had
in his house, which caused them to withdraw."*

Many people attributed the massacre to Seminoles who
lived in a Maroon in the hinterlands east of the Bradley farm. It
was reported that the Indians were seeking revenge for Captain
Bradley killing the brother of a Seminole Chief named Tiger Tail
during the First Seminole War, some twenty years earlier.
However, Mrs. Bradley swore that she heard the voice of a white
man who seemed to be directing the movement of the attackers.
Whatever the reason for the attack, there was growing unrest
between both the remaining Seminoles, who were being pushed
farther south by the Army, and freed Negro slaves who had
taken refuge with the Indians. Tensions were high among
Cracker settlers who were on the alert for the possibility of
further attacks by the Seminoles.

The Beckhams were particularly worried because their
homestead was between Durbin Swamp that lay to the north
and west of their farm and the swampy peninsula to the east that
was once the Mount Pleasant rice plantation of British Governor
James Grant. That was just the kind of hinterland that the
Seminoles preferred, both for their maroons or communities and
as refuges after attacking white settlements. On several
occasions, Adam had been hunting with his son Tucker in the
swamp when they came across what seemed to be moccasin
tracks, suggesting the recent presence of Indians.

By 1856, several thousand Seminoles had been
relocated (voluntarily or involuntarily) to the Oklahoma
Territory out west. However, hundreds of Seminoles and freed
Negroes remained in central and southern Florida hinterlands,
mainly swamps that were almost impenetrable. Further,
sporadic Indian attacks had occurred even in northern areas
thought to be safe for settlers. Consequently, the Army had once
more intervened and some people were calling the current
conflict the Third Seminole War.

Jessie and his son Tucker crushed an ample supply of French Mulberry leaves and rubbed them over the exposed parts of their bodies. That meant mostly their hands, face and neck because like most everyone in Cracker country they wore clothing that covered their bodies as much as possible. There was no other practical defense against the biting insects and blazing sun that otherwise tortured them when they were outdoors, where, in fact, they spent most of their lives. They also rubbed a liberal amount of the insect repelling leaves over their hunting dog 'Stubby.' The twenty-five pound brown and white mixed-breed hound received that unflattering name because it lost half of its tail in a tangle with a black bear a few years ago. The dog was as tough as nails, however, and would relentlessly chase after a wounded deer until it wore the poor creature out. Then it would howl to signify its position and wait for Jessie or Tucker to catch up and finish off the deer with one more shot.

Jessie and Tucker were after wild hogs today, however. They had more than enough venison smoked and stored back at the cabin. The immediate need was for hog fat that the women needed to make lye soap, which was a monthly ritual at the homestead. There were three main ingredients necessary to make lye soap: lye, tallow and water. The first ingredient, lye, was made by taking ash from the cabin's fireplace and putting it in a wood hopper like a barrel or a trough made in the form of a "V." Rainwater filtered down through the ash leaching out the alkaline salts. The solution would then be drained from the bottom of the barrel or trough.

Tallow was made by slowly boiling animal fat, in this case fat from butchered wild hogs. It required six to seven hours at a slow boil for the fat to be properly rendered. At that point, the rendered fat was dark with small bits of "cracklins," which are fried bits of meat and grizzle. The cracklins and any other impurities are filtered out when the melted mixture is strained through cheesecloth. Then the clear tallow grease was poured into bottles and allowed to stand until it turned white. By the way, the Beckham family, like most Crackers, enjoyed eating cracklins.

The final process was to blend melted tallow with the lye solution and water. Millie and Ellen had their own mix ratio handed down from their mothers for this step. The mix was covered and slow boiled for an hour or so until the consistency of pudding. It was then poured into soap molds and allowed to cool. Cracker women hated this hot, smelly and even dangerous process. However, they had no other choice; soap was generally not commercially available. In any event, the resulting soap was a very good cleaner and could be thinly shaved to dissolve in washtubs while water was being heated to wash clothes – an arduous weekly event.

The two Beckham hunters waited until mid-day to head out toward Durbin Swamp, where they knew wild hogs were sure to be resting. They brought along a mule to haul back any hog they might kill. That was necessary because Durbin Swamp was an hour's hike from the Beckham cabin and was not to be mistaken for the smaller patches of Diego swamp that bordered the Beckham homestead. Durbin Swamp was large and covered many hundreds of acres. Like many wild animals, wild hogs preferred to forage after the heat of the day had passed. That meant the best hunting time for them was late afternoon or early evening. Before then, they would be hunkered down in the shade resting near a source of freshwater. Durbin Swamp was fed by several freshwater springs, so it was an ideal haven for the hogs.

Wild hogs are filthy creatures. They rut and wallow in dirt, swamp muck and everything in between. The product of at least two hundred years of interbreeding between open range domestic hogs and Eurasian swine, they are large, mean and smell awful. That is why Jessie's strategy was to remain downwind when he entered the swamp. He and Tucker would be able to smell the creatures long before they became aware of the hunters' presence. One challenge was to keep their hunting dog, Stubby, from getting too impatient. The hogs spook faster than white tailed deer and a premature move by Stubby could bring the hunt to a speedy, unsuccessful conclusion.

Patience paid off! Toward late afternoon, the scent of wild hogs wafted downwind toward the hunters; actually, Stubby was the first to detect the scent. Jessie noticed the remnant of his tail begin to quiver and the dog frequently looked up to him in obvious anticipation. Armed with 1850 Mississippi .54 percussion rifles, Jessie and Tucker quietly followed their noses until they could see a lone boar resting comfortably on a patch of dry hammock. Both rifles were primed and loaded. They each would have only one shot. The Mississippi's were muzzle-loaded rifles and would have to be reloaded after each firing. If they missed, the hog would be gone and away in a flash.

They closed to within twenty yards of the boar and then it was over in a moment. Jessie gave the signal and both he and Tucker rose and fired simultaneously. The boar did not have a chance. It shuddered as two .54 caliber lead balls ripped into its 200-pound body. That was it. Stubby ran ahead to confirm the kill and waited for Jessie and Tucker to join him. It was too late to even think about slaughtering the hog on site. Therefore, the next step was to cut down several strong saplings and make a travois or litter to drag the hog out of the swamp to where Jessie had tethered the mule. Once they reached the mule, Jessie let the beast take over the heavy work.

It was now dusk and they were within an easy quarter mile of home. Suddenly, from the direction of the cabin, they heard the sound of a musket being fired. "My God! Your maw, Aunt Ellen and Tammy!" Jessie shouted to Tucker excitedly. Abandoning the mule and its load, Jessie, Tucker and Stubby took off at a fast run toward the cabin, reloaded Mississippi's at the ready.

***

During the day, most Cracker women spent their time outside of their houses. They made lye soap and boiled clothes clean in large kettles supported over a fire. There was usually a smoke rack for curing meats, including game, over a fire pit near the house and most cooking was done over a fire pit under an open lean-to structure that had a thatched roof. The well or other water source was also outside. Because of this, the Cracker cabin, itself, was sparsely furnished.

In the case of a double-pen, dogtrot cabin, such as the Beckman's home, one pen or side of the covered dogtrot (the passage between the two pens or halves of the cabin) would be the main living quarters. There would be an open fireplace on one outside wall. Near that wall would be a rough-hewn table with benches. A counter with cabinets below and above to store kitchenware would be against the opposite wall and at the other end of the room. There were also be a couple of chairs or so around the fireplace and one or more beds at the far end of the room. The large wrap-around, covered porch was furnished with several chairs, including rocking chairs, and at one end or side one could find a clutter of things that could not conveniently be stored elsewhere e.g. garden tools, kettles, unassembled bed frames and a lot of things that one might consider to be "junk." The second side of the cabin was usually used as a bedroom and for more storage.

While Jessie and Tucker were out in the swamp hunting, Millie, Ellen and Tammy were performing domestic chores. Young Tammy was already proficient in sewing, so her mother assigned her the task of darning socks and patching tears on clothes. The two adult women spread a quilt they were working on over the wood dining table. That way, they could sit on opposite sides of the quilt as they sewed colorful, square patches on the quilt's cotton backing.

Dusk was rapidly approaching. Even though all of the windows were open and the peak heat of the day had passed, it was still hot and humid. A light afternoon breeze occasionally flowed into the cabin; however, if failed to give much relief from the heat. Jessie and Tucker were expected back before dark. Millie knew they would be hungry and was concerned about what to prepare for dinner.

"It's almost too hot to cook a meal," Millie opined. "I wonder if we should just have grits and beans for dinner."

"Umm, there's still a quarter side of salted pork on the rack. We don't need to cook that," Ellen said. "But, if we're going to have grits and beans, we need to throw them in the kettle now. They'll take a good hour of boiling them over the fire before they're ready."

"Well, at least the smoke from the fire will help keep these darn 'skeeters' away," Ellen said, referring to the mosquitos that always plagued them beginning at dusk. "Tammy, honey, be a good girl and get a fire started in the pit outside. And, be sure to use the punk wood. Skeeters hate punk wood smoke."

Tammy was sitting on a stool by the fireplace trying to salvage one of Tucker's socks. "Mommy, this is so hard," she said. "Tell Tucker not to make such big holes in his socks." Then she put the sock still stuffed with a wood darning egg, a needle and thread dangling from it, down and began walking toward the door. Suddenly, she froze, staring at the front facing window.

"What is it, honey?" Millie asked as she looked up toward the window. Before Millie could react, Ellen screamed, followed by Millie who screamed even louder.

47

Peering at them through the open window was the painted face of a dark-skinned Seminole warrior. The Indian was dressed in a multi-colored shirt that stopped at the top of his breechcloth. A red-checkered bandana with a black feather in the back was wrapped around his head and a double strand of shell beads hung from his neck, decorating his chest. Although he might not have been more than thirty years old, his well-weathered face was deeply furrowed and he was missing most of his teeth. To the Beckham women he was a terrifying sight.

Millie spun and lunged for the 1825 Springfield musket hanging over the fireplace that was always kept primed and loaded. Ellen ran over to the room's only coat rack where a percussion revolver was secured in a leather holster hanging on one of the rack's pegs. Observing all of this, the Seminole waved his hands frantically and pointed to his mouth saying the word "food." However, Millie raised the musket toward the window and the Seminole ducked just as she pulled the trigger. The thundering report of the musket being fired was accompanied by Millie being thrown half way across the room by the weapon's recoil. Meanwhile, Tammy opened the door leading to the dogtrot and walked outside.

"Tammy!" Millie screamed as she ran after the ten-year old girl. Not realizing that she had forgotten to reload the musket, she ran after Tammy, still holding the musket that she pointed ominously at the Seminole. Ellen followed holding the revolver in front of her, not sure whether it was loaded or not. The Seminole staggered back from the cabin and stood next to a Seminole woman dressed in a wide, flouncy yellow skirt with an embroidered swath of red cloth at the bottom and a multi-colored blouse.

"Look mama," Tammy said. "She's holding a baby."

The male Seminole and his woman were terrified. The man kept pointing to his mouth and then to his wife and the child saying, "Food, want food." Both Millie and Ellen kept their weapons aimed at the Seminoles. Tammy, however, calmly walked over to the Seminole woman who showed her the baby that had to be only a few months old. Just then, Jessie and Tucker came running toward them from the woods beyond the shed where barrels of turpentine were stored. When they saw Millie and Ellen pointing weapons at the Indians, they halted, raised their own rifles and slowly advanced toward the cabin.

Chapter Seven

THE PRESIDENTIAL ELECTION of 1856 was largely about slavery versus abolition. There were three political parties at the time. The Democrats controlled the southern states. Their candidate was James Buchanan, America's ambassador to the United Kingdom. The Republicans held the edge in the northern states, backing John C. Freemont, a former Democrat and soldier who left the Democrat Party to join the Republicans. The third presidential candidate was Millard Fillmore, who had already been President of the United States from 1851 through 1853. Fillmore's political party, called the American Party, was often referred to as the "Know Nothing" Party because party members were told to say "I know nothing," when asked about their party's negative stance against immigration and the Roman Catholic Church.

The central issue during the 1856 election was the maintenance of the free versus slave compromises in which certain states (mostly in the north) were allowed to abolish slavery while other states (mostly in the south) were allowed to continue as slave states. Another major issue was the southern states insistence that runaway slaves – including those escaping to other states – be returned to their owners. Buchanan and the Democrat party won the 1856 election; thereby strengthening the institution of slavery in the southern states. This prompted an additional flurry of runaway slaves from Alabama, Georgia and the Carolinas who crossed into Florida en route to either Andros Island in the Bahamas or to the enclave of runaway slaves in the central Florida wilderness populated by the Seminole Indians.

One other enclave continued to be a refuge for runaway slaves, free blacks and maroons or Black Seminoles who were the product of intermarriage between Negroes and Creek Indians. This was the 700 square mile Okefenokee Swamp, an extensive and almost impenetrable wilderness. The United States Army built forts around the perimeter of the Okefenokee in an attempt to capture the Seminoles and force them to relocate to a reservation in the Oklahoma Territory. However, a band under the leadership of a Seminole known as Billy Bowlegs remained deep inside the swamp until well after the Third Seminole War. The hapless Seminole family that unexpectedly arrived at the Beckham homestead had been part of Billy Bowleg's clan.

***

Tammy looked at her mother, who was still pointing a musket at the terrified Seminole family, and then at the Indian woman and her baby. Before Millie could react further, Tammy asked the woman if she could hold the baby. The woman looked at her husband, who simply nodded, and then gently passed the infant to Tammy, who cooed with delight as she took the baby from its mother's arms. As she held the child, the tension of the moment seemed to be lifted. Tammy turned toward both her mother and aunt to show them the baby. Weapons that a moment earlier had been pointed at the Seminoles in a threatening manner were now lowered, including the Mississippi's held by Jessie and Tucker.

Upon scrutiny, the Beckhams could see that the family in front of them seemed to be exhausted. Despite their colorful appearance, their clothes were heavily soiled and tattered. They were clearly hungry. The male spoke hesitantly, both because his English was poor and because he was fearful for the safety of his wife and child.

"Me Joseph Red Eagle," he said pointing to himself. Then he pointed to the woman, who upon closer notice was considerably younger than he seemed to be, and said, "She Anna Morning Dove." Lastly, he pointed to the baby, now being held and rocked by Tammy, and said, "He Little Fox."

Jessie was still suspicious. He kept his rifle at the ready and then asked, "What do you want?"

"Food. Please food," The Indian named Joseph said, plaintively.

Then the baby began to cry and Tammy handed it back to its mother. Meanwhile, Ellen and Millie spoke up and said that it was clear that the Indians were not armed so they could hardly be a threat to anyone. Jessie seemed to be uncertain. He said there could be other Seminoles waiting in the woods or swamp and the family standing in front of them might just be decoys. Nonetheless, all of the Beckhams decided that Joseph, Anna and Little Fox were most likely what they seemed to be: exhausted and hungry Indians who were running away from something and who were in need of help. Therefore, Millie instructed them to sit out on the porch while she and Ellen prepared something for them to eat. Jessie and Tucker remained on the porch with them, rifles in hand "just in case."

While the women were putting together a meal for Anna and Joseph, Jessie tried to learn where they were from and where they were going. Fortunately, Anna spoke somewhat better English than her husband, who spoke a combination of creole and English called Gullah. Anna told Jessie that both of her parents were Creeks, as was Joseph's father. His mother, however, had been a runaway slave. Anna said that after their

53

parents died, she and Joseph joined Chief Billy Bowleg's clan on an island in the middle of the Okefenokee Swamp.

It had been rumored that there was a large Seminole village somewhere in the swamp that was a refuge for a clan of Creek Indians, runaway slaves and maroons or Black Seminoles. The clan was trying to avoid either being returned to their former masters or being forcibly relocated to the Oklahoma Territory. However, no white person had ever located such an island. In an attempt to prevent any of Chief Billy Bowleg's clan from escaping from the swamp, the Army surrounded its perimeter with military outposts. According to Joseph, a few days ago, soldiers moved into the swamp to engage the Seminoles. However, because they knew the swamp intimately, almost all of the Seminoles escaped. Joseph, Anna and Little Fox were among those who successfully evaded the soldiers.

Meanwhile, Millie and Ellen decided that it was too late to prepare the meal they had intended for the family because it would take too long to build a fire under the outdoor kettle and boil beans and grits. Therefore, they simply served cold slices of smoked bacon, corn bread with lard accompanied by tomatoes and onions - a tasty and sufficient meal. The family and the Indians took the meal on the front porch. While they were eating, Anna nursed Little Fox, much to the wide-eyed amazement of Tammy, who had never seen an infant being nursed, and to the embarrassment of Tucker.

The presence of the unexpected guests presented Jessie with a dilemma. They seemed to be peaceful, likely presenting no threat to the family. However, how could he be sure? Assuming they presented no threat, what should be done about them? Should he simply turn them away after they were fed? Jessie knew that the federal and state governments were trying to force all Seminoles to immigrate to the Oklahoma Territory. If he turned them away they would surely soon be captured and forced to endure relocation. That really was not his problem, he thought. But then, Millie and Ellen beckoned Jessie to join them where they could not be heard by the Indians, Millie spoke up and said, "Jessie, we can't just turn them away. They need our help – especially Anna and the baby."

"Besides, Jessie, think about it," Ellen said. "We are such a small family and you have only one son." Millie looked down, feeling bad that she was not able to have more children. "There is so much work to be done here on our farm," Ellen added, "and there is only you and Tucker to do the men's work."

Jessie knew Ellen was correct. It was not hard to guess what she was getting at. There was far more work to be done than he and Tucker could really handle: clearing the land, tilling the fields, planting and harvesting, tapping the pine trees for sap and then making turpentine and rosin, hunting, tending to the few animals they had, repairing the buildings and so much more.

"Are you two thinking what I am thinking?" he asked.

"Yes," Millie answered while Ellen nodded in agreement. "It would be a big help to all of us if we let them stay here. I think they would be very good workers."

"I am not sure how we could do that without causing a problem for ourselves, though," Jessie wondered. "If we got caught harboring runaways we might be in big trouble."

"If anybody asks, why don't we just tell them the truth – most of it, anyway," Ellen suggested. "They simply turned up on our farm and we hired them to work for us. We don't know anything about them being runaways. They are just hired hands."

"I think we are making this more of a problem than it is," Millie said. "Let's just hire them temporarily to work for us in exchange for letting them stay here and giving them food. We don't even yet know if they would be good workers."

"Yes, that make sense," Jessie said. "Besides, hardly anyone stops here at the landing except the boys from the sawmill on their way to or from St. Augustine. We could just keep the three of them out of sight when anyone is here."

"The only thing the boys from the sawmill are interested in is your Cracker Landing Lightning," Millie said smiling. "I don't think we have to worry about them."

"So, what do you think, Jessie?" Ellen asked.

Jessie looked at the two women, shook his head and then smiled. "I sure hope we don't regret this." Then the three Beckhams returned to the porch to present their idea to the Seminole couple.

Chapter Eight

THE QUIET BEAUTY OF another late summer morning at Cracker Landing was shattered by a loud shrieking sound that came from the direction of the Tolomato River. Millie and Ellen, who had been tiding up the cabin, rushed out on the wraparound porch to see what was happening. Tammy had been feeding the chickens near the hen house. She dropped the bag of cracked corn she had been carrying and ran to join her mother and aunt, while the chickens scurried to take shelter in the crawl space under the cabin. Startled but expressionless, Anna looked up from milking the cow; however, Little Fox, secured in the cradle board on his mother's back, continued to sleep soundly.

Jessie, Tucker and Joseph were in the woods to the west of the homestead tapping pine trees and pouring the sap in wood barrels. When they heard the shrill noise, all three ran as fast as they could to the cabin to make sure that the women were all right. Then, they headed to the landing where the sound came from. When they arrived at the landing, Jessie could not believe his eyes. Coming toward the landing from upriver was a barge clearly loaded with cut lumber from the sawmill. Two men Jessie recognized were standing on the bow waving at them. However, sitting on the barge deck toward the stern was what seemed to be a boiler and smoke stack, the latter pumping dark black smoke into the air. Jutting from behind the barge's stern was a paddle wheel that had to measure eight feet in diameter and half the width of the twenty-foot craft. Just then, there was another shrill sound that Jessie now recognized was a steamboat whistle. The vessel slowed as it approached the landing's pier and one of the deck hands threw Jessie a line that he quickly fastened to a cleat at the forward end of the pier.

"Howdy Jessie," Amos Peabody said as he jumped on to the pier and fastened the barge's stern line to another cleat. "How do you like our new boat?"

Amos invited Jessie and Tucker aboard the barge and introduced them to the vessel's captain, Bart Robinson, a tough-looking middle-aged man who sported a full beard. "Our captain prefers to be called either Captain Bart or just plain Bart," Amos said. Then he introduced the other deckhand, a burly Irishman named Shane. Although the barge had a full load of lumber being taken to St. Augustine, there was ample room on either side of the piles of wood to allow a person to walk from bow to stern single file. Jessie and Tucker followed Amos to the stern where they encountered the first steam engine they ever saw.

The contraption consisted of a boiler, a large cylinder with a tight-fitting piston and a heavy-duty crank and connecting rod. Amos explained that steam from the boiler was piped to the cylinder forcing the piston to move forward giving motion to the crank and connecting rod. The rod was connected to a cam on the side of the paddle wheel, thus converting forward and reverse motion to rotary motion that turned the paddle wheel. Both of Amos' guests were awed by the technology they were witnessing.

"So now," Amos continued, "We do not have to worry about the tide and river currents. We can go upriver or downriver whenever we want at any time of day. Moreover, we can cruise at four to five miles per hour meaning that even with the current against us we can easily make a round trip from the mill to St. Augustine in one day."

"But, at low tide wouldn't there be some parts of the river that are too shallow for a boat this size to pass?" Jessie asked.

"No sir," Amos replied. "This here barge only draws one foot of water. Even at low tide, the shallowest part of the river is still over three feet deep. The only thing we have to worry about is whether Willie is keeping the boiler stoked with coal," Amos added pointing to a Negro deckhand shoveling coal into the furnace at the base of the boiler.

By this time, the Beckham women, accompanied by Joseph and Anna, had decided to see what was happening at the landing and were now standing on the pier.

"Howdy, Millie and Ellen," Amos said. Then he spotted the Indians and said, "Whoa! What do we have here?"

Jessie would definitely have preferred to deal with the Indian situation at another time. However, he knew that sooner or later somebody stopping by the landing would spot them. I guess now is as good a time as any, he thought, as Captain Bart and Shane looked at the unfolding scene.

"Amos, those are our hired hands. I needed additional help to work the farm and they came along just at the right time," he said. "Which brings up a question. Are you planning to make a return trip to the sawmill later today?"

Captain Bart spoke up, "That's my intention, Jessie. It's only 8:45 a.m. now and the trip to St. Augustine from here will take about three hours. Allowing two or three hours to unload the lumber and take on supplies for the mill, we should easily be back here before dusk."

Jessie asked if they had room for all of them, including the Indians, to ride along downriver and back. If there is going to be a problem because of the Indians he might as well deal with it now, he thought. Captain Bart told him they were all welcome but they would have to leave in no more than a half hour. The women ran back to the cabin to change clothes while Jessie, Tucker and Joseph ran to the storage shed to retrieve a half dozen barrels of turpentine and rosin which they loaded onto the barge with the help of Amos and Shane. The women, including Tammy and Anna, quickly returned with a basket of cold meat and fruit that would suffice the family for the excursion. At precisely 9:15 a.m., Captain Bart sounded the barge's steam whistle. Lines were cast off and the barge, with all of its cargo and passengers, pulled away from the Cracker Landing pier and sailed downriver toward St. Augustine. The family hound, Stubby, stood on the now empty pier howling his displeasure at being left behind.

***

By the mid-nineteenth century, St. Augustine was already past its era of prime importance. In the seventeenth and eighteenth centuries, while Florida was mostly under Spanish control, the city thrived, being one of only two Florida ports – the other was Pensacola – that engaged in trade in the Caribbean and Mexico. During the nineteenth century, however, Pensacola, Apalachicola and Tampa all surpassed St. Augustine as major commercial ports. With the advent of the steamboat, even Jacksonville had become a more important port than St. Augustine. One exception, though, was marine stores including pine tar, rosin and turpentine which were shipped in large quantities from the 'Ancient City' to Georgia and the Carolinas, thereby helping to sustain the city's economic viability.

As the former capitol of Spanish La Florida and later of British East Florida, St. Augustine's central plaza was encircled by important commercial and government buildings, including the Government House and St. Johns County Probate Court. Protecting the city, and located immediately outside of the 'Ancient City's fortified walls, the former Castillo de San Marcos, built by the Spanish the previous century, had been renamed Fort Marion and had been occupied by The United States Army since 1821. Extending from the fort for nearly a mile along the city's waterfront was a coquina seawall completed by the Army Corps of Engineers in 1840. A twenty-meter wide opening in the seawall allowed utility boats and tenders to load and offload cargo from the coastal packets that were anchored in the harbor. The cargo was brought ashore at the Customs House immediately next to the Public Market, also called the Slave Market, at the eastern or harbor edge of the plaza. Fortunately, the narrow, shallow draft sawmill barge was easily able to maneuver among the boats in the boat basin and beach itself within only a few yards of the market.

In the late 1850's, there were very few indigenous people left in St. Augustine. So, there were many stares from passersby when Jessie, his family and the Indians, dressed in the colorful clothing of the Seminoles, debarked the barge and walked over to the market. Jessie's first stop was to speak with one of the merchants with whom he had previously done business to arrange for the sale of the half-dozen barrels of turpentine and rosin that he brought with him on the barge. He was disappointed to learn that the market price of a barrel of turpentine had dropped by ten cents from the time he made his previous sale. The market price for crude turpentine was now $5.02 per barrel wholesale. Having no other choice, Jessie agreed to the price. After deducting the merchant's ten percent commission, Jessie was left with $27.11. Still, that was more than enough to buy what supplies were needed on this trip to town.

While Jessie was dealing with the turpentine merchant, Millie, Ellen and Tammy decided to visit the shops in the plaza area. With a population of over 1,900 people, St. Augustine was the fifth largest city in Florida and the second largest on Florida's east coast, having only 200 people less than Jacksonville. Because of its size and the fact that it was the seat of St. Johns County, the 'Ancient City' offered residents and visitors an array of shops including drapers, milliners, cobblers, coopers, dry goods and much more. For Cracker women like Millie and Ellen, this would be an exciting afternoon.

Captain Bart told Jessie that he planned to depart for the return trip to the mill no later than 2:45 p.m. Jessie knew, therefore, that he had best be about his business quickly. Without telling the women what he had in mind, Jessie headed toward the impressive Government House at the west end of the plaza. Among its other functions, the Government House was where the circuit and probate courts were located. People stopped and stared as Jessie entered the Clerk of Court's office accompanied by a colorfully dressed Seminole Indian man and woman, the latter carrying an infant secured on a paddleboard strapped to her back.

It was common for plantation owners and merchants to have business in the courts and be accompanied by their Negro slaves. However, Seminole Indians were a rare sight and because of the open warfare between white settlers, the Army and the Seminoles, it was not surprising that their presence made some people feel uncomfortable. Only twenty years earlier, over 200 Seminole warriors, including their war leader Osceola had been tricked into attending a false peace parley at Fort Peyton seven miles south of St. Augustine where they were surrounded and captured by soldiers under the command of General Thomas Jessup. They were then incarcerated within Fort Marion, the former Castillo de San Marcos.

Jessie approached the Clerk of Court who was seated at a desk covered with files and papers. He waited patiently for the elderly man to look up, but finally he was forced to say, "Excuse me, sir."

Annoyed that his work was being interrupted, the clerk said, still without looking up, "What do you want?"

Bluntly and undiplomatically, Jessie blurted out, "I hired these people here to work on my farm. Do you folks have any problem with that?"

That finally commanded the clerk's attention. He sat back in his chair, surveyed the scene in front of him and said, "Well, I'll be damned. Are you telling me that these Indians are your employees?"

Slightly subdued, Jessie responded in a less aggressive manner, "Yes sir, that is what I am saying."

"What is your name, sir?" the Clerk of Court asked.

"Jessie Beckham and I own a farm at what everyone calls Cracker Landing."

"Cracker Landing. I have heard of that place. Upriver near the sawmill, correct?"

"Yes sir," Jessie responded now much more civilly.

"Mr. Beckham, the county doesn't much give a damn who you hire. However, some years ago, the United States Congress passed something called the Indian Removal Act. The law is that all Indians here in Florida must be relocated to the Oklahoma Territory. Unless my eyes deceive me, the man and woman standing behind you are Indians – more particularly Seminoles, who, by the way, at this moment are warring against the United States of America."

Tucker looked first at his father then at Joseph and Anna. Jessie seemed to be devastated. He knew he had just made a terrible mistake. He should have left Joseph and Anna back at the homestead where they were relatively safe. Instead, he essentially delivered them to the authorities who would send them to Oklahoma against their will. By the look on their faces,

Tucker could see that the two Seminoles also sensed that something was going badly for them. Then Jessie spoke up.

"Sir, isn't there something that can be done? These Indians are not a danger to anyone. All they want to do is to live in peace. They have been on my farm for over a month and both of them have proved that they are very good workers."

The Clerk of Court studied Joseph and Anna carefully. "How did you come by them?" he asked Jessie.

Jessie told the court official exactly what happened, including the part about Joseph and Anna escaping from the Okefenokee.

"So then, as I understand it," the Clerk of Court said, "the Indian you call Joseph is actually a maroon or what some folks call a Black Seminole."

"I don't understand," Jessie responded, bewildered at what the Clerk of Court was getting at.

"Let me put it this way," the Clerk of Court explained. "Your man Joseph's mother was a runaway slave. According to the law, any offspring of a slave becomes a slave as well – unless the slave, his mother, had been freed, which had not occurred.

"Therefore," he continued, "you essentially captured an escaped slave."

Jessie was very confused. He was about to speak when the Clerk of Court cut him off. "Let me finish," the man said.

"According to a law called the Fugitive Slave Act of 1850, if a person captures an escaped slave whose master is unknown, that person has the right to claim the slave as his own."

Jessie was just beginning to see where this was headed and began to say, "You mean that I..."

"That's right, son," the court official said. "You have two choices. One is that you can turn the two Indians and their baby over to the court, which will hand them over to the Army for mandatory relocation. Alternatively, you can claim them for yourself. If you decide on the latter all you need to do is to register their names and some other information right here and pay the court one dollar for each of them; the baby is excluded."

Jessie was jubilant! Tucker beamed and Joseph and Anna breathed a sigh of relief.

"There's just one more thing," the court official added. Jessie and the others looked up with alarm. "If you claim them for yourself, you have to personally register as their guardian."

"What does that mean?" Jessie asked.

"It means you agree that you will personally be responsible for any damages they might cause others and/or crimes they might commit. If that happens, you can be personally sued by the aggrieved."

All it took was one glance at the pitiful look on the faces of Joseph, Anna and Tucker. "I agree to that, sir," Jessie said, not fully understanding the potential liability he had just accepted.

The next few minutes were spent answering certain questions asked by the Clerk of Court as the elderly man prepared a statement for Jessie to sign. When the statement was completed and signed, Jessie paid the required court fee of one dollar for each Indian and for a moment remained standing in front of the Clerk of Court uncertain what to do next.

"Wait one minute," the Clerk of Court said. "Beckham. Umm." He turned to his assistant and said, "Ronald. I seem to recall a letter or something that arrived here a week or so ago for a Beckham. Would you please check on that?"

"Of course sir," the assistant said. A few minutes later, he returned with an envelope. "Are you Mr. Jessie Beckham at Cracker Landing?" he asked.

"I am, sir," Jessie replied as he took the letter from the Clerk of Court's assistant. Oh my Lord, he muttered to himself. It's from Samuel.

"Do you have any other business with the court today, Mr. Beckham?" the Clerk of Court asked.

"Uh, no sir," Jessie replied.

"Well then, if you do not mind, I am very busy. Good day, sir," the court official said.

With that brusque dismissal, Jessie and his small entourage wheeled out of the courthouse still somewhat unsure about what had just transpired.

They found Millie and Tammy coming out of Perpall's Dry Goods and Grocery Store that was located next to Trinity Episcopal Church across Constitution Plaza on King Street.

Jessie asked, "Where is Ellen?"

"Oh, Captain Bart invited her to accompany him on a stroll along the waterfront," Millie said. "I am sure Ellen is in good hands." Jessie raised his eyebrows and replied slowly, "I am sure she is."

Jessie directed Joseph and Tucker to shoulder the supplies Millie bought at Mr. Perpall's store and the group headed back to the waterfront. On the way, they stopped at the drapers shop where Millie bought several yards of patterned calico, cotton and light canvas so that when they returned to Cracker Landing the women could make new dresses for themselves and work pants for the men. Anna balanced the bundle of cloth on top of her head and they proceeded to the waiting barge. As they passed the open Public Market, they spotted Captain Bart and Ellen seated on a bench together chatting and laughing, obviously enjoying each other's company.

On the return trip to Cracker Landing, Jessie opened the letter from Samuel. He had not heard from his brother in several years – since their parents died, actually. He read the letter, then crumpled it in his hand.

"Jessie, what is the matter?" Millie asked.

"When I was at the Clerk of Court's office he gave me a letter sent by Samuel several weeks ago. It's bad news."

Millie looked at him with apprehension. "What news, Jessie? What's wrong?"

"Samuel's wife Rebecca died of dysentery several months ago. Their only child, a son they named William, is in the Army out in Oregon Territory fighting Indians. So, Samuel is struggling to work his farm by himself."

"How terrible," Millie said. "Why doesn't he come out here and at least be with family?"

"Actually, he said he thought of that but he really wants to keep the farm. However, equally important, he said that there are a lot of politicians in Tallahassee who are saying that Florida should really be an independent republic and not part of the Union. He said the big issue is State's rights versus the federal government and also the issue of slavery. He wondered what we are hearing in this part of Florida."

"We really do not hear much gossip upriver here at the landing," Millie said. "However, I cannot imagine there is anything to that kind of talk."

"I agree. What we do down here in the south is our business – not that of the federal government," Jessie opined. "Personally, I do not care for the idea of slavery. However, I am not an abolitionist, either. As for Florida becoming an independent republic, that is garbage talk. Heck, we just became a state not that long ago. Whatever Samuel is hearing is absolute nonsense!"

"Jessie, you really should write to Samuel and tell him how sorry we are to hear about the passing of Rebecca," Millie suggested. "You could also let him know that folks out here are not concerned about Florida leaving the Union."

Jessie didn't actually answer Millie. He fidgeted a bit, got up and said he had to talk to Captain Bart about something. Millie smiled. She knew that she would have to be the one to write a letter to Samuel. Jessie's home schooled third grade education had given him only the most basic skills of reading, writing and arithmetic. It was very difficult for him to put his thoughts down on paper.

Although Millie had almost finished grade school, there were some things she also had difficulty expressing in writing. One of them, to be sure, was the matter Samuel mentioned about people debating whether Florida, and likely other southern states, too, should secede from the Union. That thought disturbed her greatly. Millie had a premonition that if such a thing ever came about, the dissension between the northern and southern states might lead to very bad things happening. She quickly put those things out of her mind by turning to Anna and asking if she could hold the baby.

Chapter Nine

MILLIE WAS THE FIRST to sense that something was wrong. It was almost midnight. The adults had been asleep since an hour after last light, which at this time of year was about 8:30 p.m. Tammy, of course, had gone to bed somewhat earlier. Although she protested that an eleven-year-old girl was practically an adult, neither her parents nor her aunt bought that argument. Millie rose from the bed she shared with Jessie, trying not to disturb his sleep. She knew he had been working extra hard clearing more land for crops they might sell to the sawmill crews when they made their regular stops at Cracker Landing. There was not a lot of tillable land near the sawmill. Therefore, the men were always eager buyers of fresh beans, corn, melons, squash and other vegetables grown on the Beckham farm – not to mention fresh eggs now that Joseph built additional henhouses.

It must be the wind, Millie thought, as she walked out onto the porch that wrapped around the house. The wind was brisk and coming from northeast. That was unusual – especially at night. Most nights there was no wind, just a dead stillness, unless a thunderstorm passed through; but, those winds usually came from the west. She looked up at the starless sky and saw fast moving dark gray clouds doing their best to obscure the half- moon that was this night's only source of light.

"You feel it, too," a voice from just inside the doorway said, more a question than a statement. It was Ellen walking onto the porch to join her sister-in-law.

Millie looked at Ellen and said, "I don't like it. Something's brewing. You can almost taste salt in the air. The wind is coming from the ocean – the northeast. That likely means trouble."

"Yes, there is a heaviness in the air, as well. Joseph and Anna must also feel it. Look across the field towards the swamp. You can see a light coming from the direction of their hut. One of them must have lit a lamp. I wonder if the baby is alright."

"I really wish they would build themselves something more substantial than just a chickee," Millie said. She was referring to the raised, thatched hut on poles that the two Indians built for themselves down by the swamp.

"Anna said that is how the Seminoles live," Ellen responded. "They seem to feel quite comfortable living in a chickee. I cannot imagine how that will work in the winter, however. But, I guess that's their problem."

"Well, meanwhile, Jessie is dead to the world, the poor dear. He is exhausted. I do not believe the roar of a bear would wake him up," Millie said.

"The same with Tucker. He's getting to be a very strong boy and seems to thrive doing a man's work. I really think he works almost as hard as ... Oh my! Did you feel that big gust of wind?" Ellen said, interrupting herself. "Anyway, as I was saying, Tucker did pretty well keeping up with Jessie clearing that last acre."

Ellen felt a tug at her nightshirt. "Aunt Ellen, please come back to bed," Tammy pleaded. "The noise of the wind scares me. Tucker said the sound of wind is really the noise

70

made by the souls of all the dead Indians roaming around the swamp."

"I'll take care of Tucker when he wakes up," Ellen said angrily. "That's just nonsense! Alright sweetheart, let's go back to bed and we'll let your mama keep an eye on the wind," she said winking at Millie.

Millie smiled at both of them and then looked back up at the sky. The dark scud clouds seemed to be moving faster and then suddenly there was a downburst of rain that drove her from the porch back in to the house. Something is absolutely not right, she thought.

***

The *Athena* shook violently as it plunged into another breaking wave five miles northeast of the relative safety of St. Augustine's harbor – if, indeed, it was still possible to navigate the harbor entrance in this storm. Ship's Captain Lloyd Hollandale swore under his breath at the miserable luck that seemed to have placed him, his ship and crew in the middle of what was becoming a full-fledged hurricane. The storm was not forecasted. However, ever since leaving his home port of Savannah, the barometer continued to plunge precipitously. It was now reading 970 millibars, fully in hurricane territory.

The *Athena* was a small, 800-ton coastal steam packet that regularly sailed between Savannah, Georgia and St. Augustine, Florida. Typically, on the outbound trip to St. Augustine, its cargo would be ceramics, cloth, coal, manufactured goods and certain foodstuffs like coffee beans, tea flour and sugar. Then, on the return trip to Savannah, Captain Hollandale would load his ship with crates of lumber, oranges, turpentine and other Naval stores needed by Savannah merchants.

The twenty-year old *Athena* had been converted to steam from sail less than ten years ago. Therefore, in addition to a single twenty-foot smokestack held upright by guy wires, the vessel still sported a forward mainmast with a gaff-rigged sail aft and a forestay and jib. Because of the high winds and mounting seas of the storm, Hollandale had ordered the gaff-rigged sail reefed. The *Athena* was now struggling to maintain course on steam power only with the jib helping to steady the ship. Its 276 horsepower steam engine, manufactured by the Randolph Elder and Company in Glasgow, Scotland, strained as the ship's single brass screw lost thrust whenever waves lifted the ship's stern high out of the water, which was becoming more frequent in this following sea.

Standing next to his boatswain, George Hawkins, in the cramped wheelhouse of the *Athena*, Hollandale knew his ship was well built, being of double oak plank construction. Still, he feared that if he lost steam power, and thus steerage, the ship might breech. Or, if one of the cargo hatches broke loose, the cargo hold could flood. In either case, there might be no way to save the ship, crew and cargo. At last, Hollandale spotted the beacon of the St. Augustine Lighthouse and gave a sigh of relief, reckoning they had only another mile or so before they would spot the buoy marking the channel into the harbor. Suddenly, Hawkins gave a cry of alarm. Against the light from the lighthouse both of the men could see a mass of white foam as the raging sea crashed against the North Breakers sandbar that ran for a half-mile outside of the harbor entrance. Before either of the men could utter another word, a massive wave lifted the *Athena* by the stern and then crashed the ship down on the sandbar sending a great shudder throughout the vessel. There was the sound of cracking timbers and an instant later seawater poured over the white-hot boiler causing it to explode, ripping the stern of the vessel apart.

***

Jessie awoke at what normally would have been daybreak. However, the storm that was raging outside of the cabin caused an eerie darkness to prevail even at this time of morning. Foregoing breakfast, Jessie stood on the cabin's porch surveying the scene before him. Stumbling toward the house against the wind were Joseph and Anna, who was carrying Little Fox against her bosom in order to shield him from the pelting rain. Jessie helped them up the stairs and then, exhausted from the struggle, the two drenched Indians and their baby huddled on the porch's leeward side seeking shelter from the wind and rain. Millie ran out onto the porch to see if there was anything she could do to help them. Tammy tagged along so she could play with Little Fox.

Haltingly, Joseph told Jessie that the wind was too great for the chickee they built and had blown off the thatch roof, exposing what little they had to the rain. He said he doubted there would be anything left of the chickee after the storm passed. Luckily, he added, it could be rebuilt with minimal effort. That was one of the reasons the Seminoles preferred that type of shelter.

The rain was so intense that it was barely possible to see the barn and corral from the porch. Well, Jessie thought, the cow, mule, hogs, goats and two plow horses would have to fend for themselves. There was not much that could be done for them in this kind of storm. However, Joseph said that in such conditions, the Indians set the animals free. He said that instinctively they would know what to do – most likely taking what shelter they could find in the woods. So, he and Jessie made their way against the wind to the barn and corral to make sure the animals were not restrained. Sure enough, without any prompting they all headed toward the woods where, hopefully, they would be collected after the storm.

The chickens were another matter, however. Abandoning the henhouses Joseph recently built for them, they all took shelter either under the cabin or on the cabin's porch, which was now getting crowded – especially on the side sheltered from the wind and in the covered dogtrot that separated the two rooms of the cabin. Normally, the family hound Stubby would not have allowed the chickens to be on the porch. However, he seemed to sense that this was an exceptional situation and tolerated their presence. He made sure they did not enter the cabin, itself, though.

The rain and wind intensified as the morning progressed. It was downright terrifying for everyone. Then the destruction began. First, the kitchen lean-to and smoking racks both disappeared in a horrendous wind gust. Next, a large live oak tree was uprooted and fell on top of the barn. With every additional gust – each so strong that it would easily knock down a grown man – some other damage could be spotted. Then the cabin, itself, began to shake. The shutter protecting the window on Ellen's side of the cabin blew off and a branch torn off a nearby tree broke the window glass allowing rain to pour into the room.

Jessie, Tucker and Joseph ran into the room and moved as much of the bedding and clothes as they could from Ellen's room to the main cabin room across the open dogtrot. The broken glass and other rain-soaked debris would have to be cleaned up later. Then, with a terrifying noise, the fireplace chimney in the cabin's only other room crashed to the ground. The combination of hurricane force winds and driving rain was simply more than the mud brick structure could withstand. The loss of the chimney was not a complete surprise to the Beckhams, however. Because many Cracker homes had been lost due to chimney fires, it was customary to build chimneys leaning outward from the house or cabin so that they could easily be knocked down away from the dwelling if they caught fire. Still, at this point, with everyone huddled together in the one dry room of the cabin, there was an overwhelming fear that further tragedy was just around the corner.

Then, suddenly, the wind began to abate and the bands of driving rain came somewhat less frequently. Two hours and many prayers later, the family and the two Indians stepped back out on the porch to survey the damage. The wind was still blowing strongly, but nowhere near hurricane force, and the rain came in spates of a shower rather than a downpour. The destruction that the hurricane had brought was now evident. Among the several outbuildings on the farm, only the tool shed remained undamaged. The remains of the outhouse, smoking rack, hen houses and cooking lean-to were scattered over a large area. The barn was badly damaged. In addition, as far as they could see, between the cabin and the woods at one end and the swamp at the other, all of the crops were gone. What had been fields of late summer vegetables was now nothing more than mud and standing water. In fact, the entire area surrounding the cabin was flooded.

"Dear Lord, Jessie!" Millie cried. "What about the landing?"

Jessie was so distraught he could hardly answer. He hugged Millie and then pulled his entire family to him. Barely able to hold back tears, himself, he said, "I fear the pier is probably gone, too. However, we have our lives and we can rebuild."

Ellen went over to the cabinet where many of the family's personal items including the bible were kept. Then, all of the Beckhams, as well as Joseph, Anna, knelt in the middle of the room. Ellen began reading verses from the bible and the small group of survivors of a terrible storm prayed in thanksgiving that their lives had been spared.

Outside, the sun began breaking through the clouds as the offshore hurricane moved north toward Brunswick, Georgia, which was already beginning to feel its effects. The 1858 late summer hurricane passed the northeast coast of Florida

75

approximately forty miles offshore. Heavy wind, pounding rain and a storm surge caused moderate damage to buildings in St. Augustine. However, Fort Marion, the former Spanish built Castillo de San Marcos, escaped unscathed because of its massive coquina construction. The storm surge sent flooding water up the tidal Tolomato River inundating forests, swamps and the handful of homesteads in the river's flood plain with brackish seawater. Luckily, the tide was ebbing when the hurricane struck, therefore by the time the surge reached Cracker Landing most if its force had dissipated. The Cracker Landing pier was damaged, but not seriously. Nonetheless, there was flood damage in a broad area of St. Augustine. Some of the structurally less well constructed Cracker farmhouses and buildings in the county were seriously damaged. Thankfully, no loss of life attributed to the storm was reported.

Chapter Ten

THE NEXT DAY, THE SUN shined brightly. It was as though all of nature was trying to dry out from the drenching storm. By mid-morning, all of the storm-soaked bedding, clothes and other linen goods had been hung on the porch railing to dry out. Broken glass from the blown out windows had been carefully picked up and the remaining glass shards were swept into the spaces between the floor planks to fall to the ground below the cabin. With the exception of the fallen chimney, major damage that would have to be repaired before the onset of winter, there was relatively little damage to the cabin itself. The men were eager, however, to learn what damage had occurred to the rest of the homestead.

Jessie and Joseph knew that when flooding occurs, such as in the previous day's storm, many woodland and swamp critters are forced out of their natural habitat as they seek higher ground. That included snakes and alligators. Jessie told Millie and the other women to remain in the cabin or on the porch. He did not want them venturing out in the area where the floodwaters were now receding for fear they might encounter an aggressive or venomous creature. Therefore, the women spent their time tidying up the cabin and trying to get everything back as it was before the storm hit. Jessie, Tucker and Joseph, on the other hand, ventured away from the cabin to take stock of the extent of the property damage.

As Jessie suspected when he surveyed the fields from the deck of the porch the previous day, the late summer crops were mostly ruined. Some ready-to-pick squash and melons could be salvaged. However, the fields would have to be tilled again and new crops had to be planted. That was not as disastrous as it might seem. Late September was a good time to plant certain crops like beets, cabbage, various greens and even tomatoes. All those crops could be harvested before the first frost in December.

When the men reached the barn, they were confronted with good and bad news. The live oak tree that fell on the barn destroyed half its roof and would be very difficult and time consuming to remove. On the other hand, half of the roof was intact and could still provide the animals with some shelter from the hot sun and rain. Even better, the small section of the barn where Jessie stored barrels of turpentine for shipment downriver seemed to be untouched by the storm and there was no damage to the tool shed. As the men were deciding repair priorities, a loud piercing whistle sounded from the direction of the river. That could only mean that the sawmill's steam barge was planning to stop at Cracker Landing.

Ellen and Millie heard the whistle, too. As soon as the whistle sounded, Ellen's eyes lit up and she began brushing back her hair. She started going down the porch stairs until Millie reminded her about Jessie's warning that the flooding might have driven alligators and snakes close to the cabin and certainly to the path leading to the landing. With that in mind, the two women, Anna and Tammy decided it would be more prudent to remain on the porch or in the cabin.

Jessie, Tucker and Joseph, on the other hand, headed for the landing – Joseph leading the way, machete in hand in case they encountered any dangerous critters. When they reached the pier, they saw that several of the pilings were leaning at an awkward angle and that the upwelling high water had badly loosened a few deck planks. Luckily, there was no major damage and what damage occurred could easily be repaired. However, securing the steam barge to the damaged pier turned out to be somewhat of a challenge. Nonetheless, after a couple tries, fore and aft lines from the barge were passed to the men standing on the pier and a spring line was successfully rigged.

"Jessie!" Captain Bart Robinson shouted. "Are all of you OK?" Millie's mother Sarah was standing next to Captain Bart looking frantic.

"Thank God we all are OK, Bart," Jessie replied. "The cabin chimney collapsed. However, other than that the cabin is in fair shape. Some of the outbuildings took quite a hit, though. That big live oak next to the barn completely uprooted and smashed the roof. But, don't you worry a bit, Sarah. Not one of us is hurt." Sarah's look of worry immediately turned to one of relief. Meanwhile, Tucker jumped up on the barge and gave his grandmother a big hug.

"We've been worried about you down here," Amos said. "The mill is mostly fine. Damn thing was built like a fort. The biggest problem was that we had to shut down the boiler, so we have no steam power for the sash and circular saws until its back up and running. We had some pier damage like you did and some of the bunkhouse windows facing east were blown out. "I'm glad as all hell that the cookhouse is OK, though," he chuckled. "I sure don't want to go without some good hot meals!" Amos was referring to the bunkhouse that was home to most of the sawmill's dozen male workers and the cookhouse adjacent to it. The mill proper was no place for women, so almost all of the men working there were single. The exception was Millie's father, Tom Sutter, who had a cabin built for him and Millie's mother Sarah

79

"Those tall pines east of the mill helped shelter us from the worst of it, I suppose," Captain Bart said. "However, back to you folks. You say that Millie, Ellen and Tammy made it through alright? I can see that young Mr. Tucker seems to be fine."

Jessie nodded. "And also Joseph, his wife Anna and their baby Little Fox," he said. "Come on up to the cabin and relax for a while. I might even find an undamaged jug of Cracker Landing Lightning! That means you, too, Willie," he added pointing at the Negro member of the crew whose job it was to keep the barge's steam boiler stoked with coal. Everyone laughed, except Joseph who was almost always stone-faced and who would not touch a drop of Lightning with a ten-foot pole.

"Before we go up to the cabin, we have some rough cut planks we thought you might need," Captain Bart said. "Tell us where you want them and we'll all pitch in and get them offloaded in just a few minutes."

"Bart, that's mighty kind of you. I have a lot of repair work to do and I sure could use them. However, there is no way I can pay for them right now."

"Not to worry, my friend. Everyone in these parts is in the same fix. You can repay the mill when your fall harvest comes in."

"Thank you very much, Bart," Jessie said appreciatively. "By the way, re-tilling the fields is a top priority. We'll be planting the fall crop sometime in the next couple of weeks. First, I want to repair the damage to the outbuildings and to the cabin, itself. Everything considered, it will be about three to four months before harvest time."

They piled the planks on the undamaged part of the pier and then everyone, including Millie's mother, started to walk up the path to the cabin. "Stop!" Joseph shouted, holding up his hand. He rushed forward, raising his machete and then halted; a

80

five-foot alligator blocked the path. The animal's mouth was
wide open and it was making a loud hissing sound. Joseph
handed the machete to Tucker and then calmly walked around
behind the alligator, which was still facing the other men, mouth
open and hissing menacingly. He grabbed the gator by the tail
and tugged it off the path into the surrounding brush where he
let it go.

"Small gator," he grunted. "No hurt nobody."

Tucker handed the machete back to Joseph. Sarah's eyes
were wide with apprehension. Jessie shook his head and the
men from the barge just looked at each other. Then, with Joseph
and his machete in the lead, they all headed for the cabin.

Jessie's cabin was built on a dry hammock five to six feet
higher than the Tolomato River. Most of the time, there was no
danger of flooding – even when a heavy storm caused the river
to rise above its normal high water mark. Unfortunately, the
hurricane caused the river to rise high enough so that it flooded
the cleared fields of Jessie's farm. However, as in most Florida
coastal areas, the farm's soil was a sandy loam that drained
standing water quickly. In fact, within just a few hours after the
rain stopped, most of the standing water had been drained into
the nearby swamp that, in turn, fed into the river. By the time
that the sawmill barge crew arrived at Cracker Landing, the path
up to the Beckham's cabin was almost dry, as were the fields
where the crops had been planted.

When the group arrived at the cabin, Millie, Ellen and
Tammy were standing on the porch waiting for them. As soon
as Millie spotted her mother, she ran down the porch steps and
the two women hugged each other. "Your father and I have
been so worried about you," Sarah said. "He would have come,
also, but there was a lot of cleanup work he had to do at the
mill." Meanwhile, Tammy quickly joined her mother and
grandmother with Ellen following close behind.

Captain Bart tipped his hat to the ladies and then surveyed the extent of the damage to the homestead. "You are going to need some help getting this put back in shape," he said as he glanced up at the porch and saw Ellen smiling at him. "If you would not mind some company this Sunday, perhaps a couple of the boys and me could drop by to give you a hand." Ellen beamed at his suggestion. Millie smiled and nodded. Jessie said he would be most grateful for any help his sawmill friends were able to provide.

Jessie invited the group to take a seat on the porch and sent Tucker to see if he could find a jug of Lightning in the undamaged part of the barn. Meanwhile, Millie asked the men if they would like a glass of clear, cool water.

"Miss Millie," Amos said, "The storm must have flooded your well and the river water is not fit to drink – dirty and brackish as it is. Y'all need to keep whatever fresh water you have for yourself."

"Not to worry Amos," Millie said. "We can make whatever fresh water we need overnight."

Amos gave Millie a blank look and she said, "Step over here to the dogtrot," she was referring to the covered area separating the two pens that made up the dogtrot cabin.

"See here," she said, pointing to a concave rock the size of a large pot hanging by a chain from a wood tripod. The bowl of the rock was filled with water. Beneath the rock was a wood bucket that was being filled with clear water steadily dripping from the curved bottom of the rock.

"Miss Millie, what in the world is that contraption?" Amos asked.

"The rock is actually lava rock from the Canary Islands that was used as ship ballast many years ago. We picked this one up in St. Augustine the last time we were there," Millie

82

explained. "The rock is fairly light and soft. The bowl shape was carved out by whoever owned it previously."

"I still do not understand," Amos said, perplexed.

"Well, lava rock is very porous and water will actually flow through it. As you can see, we simply pour water into the bowl shaped top part of the rock and after a little while it comes out of the bottom and drips into the bucket. But, as it goes through the rock, all the impurities like dirt and whatever are filtered out."

"You mean this is how you get your fresh water out here?" Amos said in disbelief.

"Not all of it," Millie answered. "If the water level in the well is up and we can draw nice clear water, we'll use that. We also collect rain water, which we prefer for washing clothes and our hair because it is nice and soft."

"Well, I'll be darned," Amos replied, watching his language in the presence of a lady. "You learn something new every day!"

No sooner had Millie and Amos returned to the front porch than Ellen said she would be happy to show Captain Bart the lava rock filter and the two of them disappeared around the corner of the dogtrot. Meanwhile, Tucker came back from the barn carrying two jugs of Lightning. Jessie said one was for use now and the second was for the barge crew to take with them in appreciation for stopping by with the wood from the mill. After about an hour Captain Bart and the barge crew continued their trip to St. Augustine. Sarah said she planned to stay with Millie and Ellen a few days to help them.

Late that afternoon, the Beckhams were all busy making what repairs they could to the homestead when most unexpectedly they heard the barge whistle sound again. Jessie and Joseph went down to the river as the barge pulled close to the pier. It was clear, however, that Captain Bart was not planning on actually stopping.

"What's up, Bart?" Jessie hollered.

"Nothing good," Captain Bart shouted in return.

"When we got down to St. Augustine there was a big crowd in the plaza and a lot of shouting and hollering going on. It seems that the last packet arriving from Savannah brought some troubling news."

"What was that?" Jessie asked apprehensively.

"There is a lot of talk in Washington about troublemakers up north pushing congress to end slavery all over the country. People down here, especially people in Georgia, the Carolinas and a lot of folks here in Florida, are pretty upset about that idea."

"What I want to know is how the hell can people in Washington tell citizens of the southern states what they can or cannot do?" Jessie demanded.

"Damned if I know," Captain Bart replied. "However, they're planning a big rally tonight in the plaza. In fact, the owner of our mill, Joe Finnegan, will be there. He'll probably stop at the mill on his way back to Jacksonville. Let's talk about it more when Amos and I come down Sunday to help y'all out."

"We'll Look forward to seeing you and Amos then, Bart," Jessie hollered as the barge pulled away.

Chapter Eleven

As DUSK FELL UPON THE CITY, the small parade ground inside St. Augustine's Fort Marion was brightly lit by flames from torches held by scores of angry town residents who had assembled to protest the latest abolition news from Washington. Brought by the afternoon packet from Savannah, and later confirmed by telegraph, the news reported the demands of northern abolitionists that slavery be prohibited in all thirty-two states of the Union. That news was met by dismay and anger among many of the residents of St. Augustine, as well as many throughout most of Florida. Those who were anti-abolitionists rejected the notion that northern politicians in Washington had a right to dictate how the southern states should conduct their business and treat their Negroes. It was all so unacceptable!

After leaving Fort Marion, the marchers proceeded through the Ancient City's northern gate to St. George Street, the city's main residential thoroughfare. They were en route to their rally point in the Plaza de Constitution. Standing on the wooden gazebo in the center of the plaza were several local politicians, including St. Augustine Mayor Paul Arneau, Joseph Finnegan and Senator David Levy Yulee, all who eagerly awaited their arrival. Behind the city notables were members of a six-piece brass band ready to strike up patriotic music as soon as the marchers appeared.

The mob continued their march down St. George Street past landmarks such as the Old School House, Dr. Seth Peck's two-story, balconied home and the stately Magnolia Hotel. Curious hotel guests lined the building's wraparound porch enjoying the sight of an impromptu parade. They reveled in gossiping about the slogans shouted by the marchers that were printed on hastily made signs:

PROTECT STATES RIGHTS!

NO UNION WITHOUT SLAVERY!

UPHOLD DRED SCOTT!

PATRIOTS YOUR STATE NEEDS YOU!

It was an emotionally charged event with marchers of every age and gender. One group was absent, however. There were no freed blacks in the crowd nor were any of the city's 136 registered slaves present. Even the slaves of homeowners on St. George Street were nowhere to be seen, choosing to remain out of sight. Several, however, peeked through shuttered windows apprehensively at the spectacle passing their masters houses.

When the first marchers reached the Catholic Church at the end of St. George Street opposite the plaza, the band on the gazebo began playing. As the crowd formed between the slave market and the gazebo, the band ran through a medley of popular southern music. Sometimes in harmony and sometimes not, the blaring melodies of a trumpet, French Horn, trombone, tuba and cornet filled the plaza from the waterfront to the Government House. The crowd was enthralled; practically everyone joined in singing the lyrics of songs such as *Old Susanna*, *My Old Kentucky Home* and the most recent popular southern song, *Dixie*. Standing on the gazebo, clapping their hands along with the crowd, Mayor Arneau, Senator Yulee and

Joseph Finnegan beamed at the size and enthusiasm of the throng before them. Then, the mayor gave a signal and the music subsided. It was now time to rally the crowd to the cause that brought all of them together – states' rights and abolition.

The crowd in front of the gazebo was still shouting and waving signs. Mayor Arneau motioned with his hands for quiet as he began to address the crowd.

"Ladies and gentlemen!" he pleaded. "Please give me your attention. I share your concerns. The sad news we received today is very troubling. That's why we are here tonight, to stand together as fellow citizens of this great and ancient city and of the great state of Florida."

Then, the mayor went on to introduce his principal guests.

"First, it is my pleasure to introduce the Honorable David Levy Yulee, United States Senator from the State of Florida, who is seated to my right." The crowd erupted with applause.

"Many of you know that Senator Yulee has a long and distinguished political career, first representing the State of Florida when it was still a Territory and now as one of its distinguished senators. He is a no nonsense man who is known among his colleagues as the Florida Fire Eater for his vocal support of slavery and states' rights. Senator Yulee, as some of you may know, is the founder of the Florida Railroad that, when completed, will extend from Fernandina on Amelia Island through Jacksonville to Cedar Key on the Gulf of Mexico. He also owns a 5,000 acre sugar cane plantation along the Homosassa River."

There was even more applause.

"Next, I have the honor of introducing one of our most distinguished citizens and the chairman of the Committee of

Vigilance and Safety of Jacksonville, Mr. Joseph Finnegan. As many of you know, Joe is the founder of Jacksonville's first sawmill and more recently built the sawmill located at the head of the Tolomato River. He is also a personal friend of our governor, Madison S. Perry, and brings an important message from the governor."

There was another round of applause from the crowd followed by the Mayor introducing a handful of other city and county officials. Then the speechmaking began. Initially, the speeches dealt with the broad issue of the rights of the thirty-two individual states versus those of the federal government. The speakers pointed out that the economy of most southern states was plantation- based, requiring far more manpower than the manufacturing-based economies of the northern states. He said that amount of manpower could only be achieved by continuing the practice of slavery. The speakers all agreed that without slavery, the entire economy of the south would collapse and that no one, most certainly not the politicians in Washington, had the right to cause the south such a calamity. Those comments were met by rousing applause accompanied by hoots and shouts and more band music.

By now, the crowd was thoroughly enraged. Their anger was heightened as Senator Yulee reported that up north there was an upstart radical named Abraham Lincoln who had ambitions for the White House. Lincoln, he said, had just completed a series of debates with his opponent Stephen Douglas, incumbent senator of Illinois. Although Douglas was reelected, by a thin margin, Lincoln won the debates with his anti-slavery rhetoric. It was clear that if he won the forthcoming 1860 presidential election, the southern states would have no choice except to secede from the Union. Now, the crowd was inflamed to the point of becoming a shouting and screaming mob. Then, Joseph Finnegan rose and conveyed his message from the governor.

"My dear friends," he said. "President Buchanan is doing everything he can to uphold the right of any state to determine whether or not slavery is appropriate for their citizens. Earlier this year he urged the United States Supreme Court to hear and decide the case of Dred Scott, a Negro slave, versus John Sanford, who claimed ownership of Scott via inheritance. The court found in favor of the Sanford. President Buchanan also urged that the Territory of Kansas be admitted to the Union as a slave state, which was approved by congress."

However, Finnegan informed the crowd that Buchanan was facing very strong headwinds and had announced that he will not run for reelection in '60 giving that radical Lincoln a good shot at the presidency. He concluded with a request passed on from the governor.

"Our beloved governor, my dear friend Madison S. Perry, believes that if Lincoln is elected in two years, Florida and the other southern states should secede from the Union. That, my fellow citizens, might mean armed conflict between the North and the South. Governor Perry is very concerned that our own state militia has fallen into disrepair, both in terms of manpower and equipment. There is not one fully staffed, fully equipped militia company in the entire state. He asked me to covey his request that the people of St. Augustine form a militia of at least 500 men and that if done, the state will provide the armament and training necessary to make that militia an effective fighting force."

The crowd went wild, with men throwing top hats in the air, patting each other on the back and hugging their women. All the while, the band played military marching and other patriotic music. It was a wondrous moment for some, but a very ominous occasion for others.

Cracker Landing

Chapter Twelve

ELLEN BECKHAM STARED AT the reflected image in the mirror hanging next to her bed in the south pen of the Beckham cabin. She was the only one in the family with chestnut colored hair. Everyone else, both the men and her mother, had hair color that ranged from light to dark brown. Ellen knew that two generations ago, the Beckhams had emigrated from Norfolk, England to Savannah, Georgia, so it was understood that all of the Beckhams were of English heritage. In fact, the surname Beckham was derived from "Becca," possibly an ancient English word for a farm instrument, and "ham," meaning homestead. Thus, in older English, Beckham meant the Becca homestead. However, because of the touch of red in her hair, Ellen's friends and family often joked that there had to be a little Irish somewhere in the family history.

It was early Sunday morning, the day that Captain Bart Robinson promised he and at least one other person from the sawmill would come to help repair the Beckham homestead at Cracker Landing. Less than a half-hour earlier, Ellen, Millie and Millie's mother Sarah had served the family a modest breakfast. Some of the stored foodstuff had been ruined in the hurricane. That included some of the meat hanging in the smoke shed and outdoor kitchen. Luckily, supplies of flour, salt, lard and cornmeal that had been stored in the cabin were untouched, as were the canned vegetables and fruits. The morning breakfast consisted of fried Johnnycakes, coffee, and some canned black berries – not bad considering the circumstances.

Now, as Ellen waited to hear the whistle signaling that the mill's steam barge was approaching, she looked at herself in the mirror primping her hair to make sure she would be as presentable as possible to Captain Bart Robinson, who seemed to have taken a fancy to her. Ellen was rapidly approaching the age of forty and had been sure that she would be a spinster for the rest of her life. Not that she was unhappy living with her brother and sister-in-law and the children. They truly had a very pleasant family life together. However, what was missing from Ellen's life was a man, other than her brother, who would love her and whom she could cherish.

It was likely far too late to think about having her own children. However, there was nothing preventing her from having a wonderful and intimate relationship with the man who would become her husband. Ellen's wandering thoughts were cut short when she heard the whistle of the steam barge. She took one more look at herself in the mirror before joining Jessie, Millie and Sarah who were walking down the porch steps on their way to the landing. She felt slightly flush. The thought of seeing Captain Bart again set her heart fluttering. He was such a handsome man!

When the small group reached the landing, they saw that Tucker had arrived first and was already helping tie up the barge to the pier. They were surprised to see not only Captain Bart and his usual crew standing on the barge, but also Millie's father Tom Sutter and two burly men who they had not previously met. Tom briskly jumped on the pier, walked over to his wife, and gave her a hug. Then, he gave a special hug to Millie who he had not seen for a few weeks.

"It's good to see you darl'n. Your maw and me were very worried about all of you during that big storm," Tom said to his daughter.

"It's good to see you, too, daddy. With all you have to do at the mill, I did not expect you to come down today. What a wonderful surprise."

"You're looking well," Tom said. "Seems that Jessie is taking good care of you."

"For sure he is, Daddy. And take a look at your granddaughter here. Tammy is getting to be such a big girl."

Tom picked Tammy up in his broad arms and said, "That she is." Then he put Tammy down, went over, put an arm around Tucker's shoulder and said, "Now here is one fine young man. You snag any gators lately, son?"

"No gators, grandpaw," Tucker replied. "But, I did blow the head off a rattler before he got Tammy," the boy said smiling from ear to ear.

"Oh my, I want to hear that story," Tom said. Then he walked over to Jessie and Ellen, hugged Ellen and shook Jessie's hand. "Jessie, we have things at the mill back to where they should be. So, I thought you would not mind if I brought along my best top man and pitman. Together with Bart and his crew we might be able to help move things along even faster today."

Sutter was referring to the two men who used a vertical whipsaw to cut a log along its length when manual sawing was necessary. The pitman was positioned in a pit below the log. His job was to pull the blade down. Whipsaws cut in only one direction – downward. The top man's job was to keep the saw blade lined up on a mark made lengthwise along the log and to pull to blade up after each downward stroke.

"Tom, this is more than we could have hoped for," Jessie said to his father-in-law. "We are very grateful for your help."

As the men were speaking, Ellen and Captain Bart exchanged a series of glances and smiles. Then, it was time to head up to the cabin and begin repairing the hurricane damage. Captain Bart instructed Amos, Shane and Willie to straighten the tilted pilings and repair the loose planks on the deck of the pier. He told them to come up to the cabin when they were finished and to bring the special supplies they had brought with them. Meanwhile, the barge captain escorted Ellen on the walk to the cabin making sure the two of them lagged a little behind the main group.

While the group made their way to the cabin, Joseph Red Eagle and his wife Anna Morning Dove were at the far end of the homestead property rebuilding their chickee. Luckily, the four main cypress log poles serving as supports for the rest of the structure were intact. Several of the more slender cypress poles frames on which the thatch roof was tied were also intact, as was the raised living platform. Unfortunately, most of the thatch roof was gone, blown away in the storm. Nonetheless, the two skilled Seminoles had been working on the chickee repair since the previous day and were now almost finished. Replacing the roof with palm branches was made relatively easy since the area was littered with braches blown off the now naked palm trees. After the chickee was repaired, Joseph set about rounding up the animals that had been set free to fend for themselves during the hurricane. The chickens were not a problem because during the storm, they had taken refuge beneath the cabin.

When the group from the barge arrived back at the cabin, Tom Sutter assigned his sawmill workers to cut up and remove the fallen live oak tree from the barn. He knew their expertise using a whipsaw would make relatively quick work of that problem. Jessie assigned the rest of the men to tackle rebuilding the outdoor kitchen, smoke shed and even the outhouse. They saved the most laborious project for last –

reconstructing the fallen chimney. Meanwhile, Stubby, the family hound, roamed from one project to another satisfying his curiosity about all of the activity that was taking place.

The original chimney was made by surrounding a tabby concrete flute with a frame of wood slats attached to the exterior of the cabin. Tabby concrete was then patched between the slats. Tabby concrete is made by mixing lime with sand, ash, broken oyster shells and water. Anticipating the need, the barge crew brought a few sacks of lime with them. All of the rest of the material was reclaimed from the original fallen chimney. It was not that the job was difficult, but rather it was time consuming. However, with all hands working on their assigned tasks, the Beckham homestead was in reasonable repair by late afternoon – time for relaxation and a good meal. The problem was that because of the storm damage much of the Beckham's food supply had been destroyed.

Repairing the Cracker Landing pier as best as they could, the barge crew lugged the supplies Captain Bart brought with him up to the cabin: a sack of beans and another of grits, a slab of bacon, a smoked ham, potatoes, squash, melon and more. Tom told Jessie he figured that they would not need milk or cheese once they rounded up the goats and cow that Jessie let roam before the storm. Jessie, Millie and Ellen were overwhelmed by Tom and Sarah's generosity. Jessie told Tucker to go and fetch Joseph and Anna to join them. Then the women began preparing what would be a grand feast for everyone.

After everyone ate their fill, Jessie built a punk wood fire in the smoke house pit to help ward off the mosquitos that were beginning to appear. Amos went back to the barge and returned a few minutes later with a fiddle. Shane took a harmonica out of his pocket and soon the air was filled with popular Cracker tunes like "Cindy," "The Girl I Left Behind," and "Turkey in the Straw:"

Turkey in the straw, hee haw haw!
Turkey in the hay, hey hey hey!
Roll 'em up and twist 'em up, a high tuck a-haw,
And hit 'em up a tune called Turkey in the Straw!

Captain Bart wasted no time. He threw his cap aside, grabbed Ellen's arm and began dancing to the music. A moment later, Jessie and Millie joined the frolic as did Tom and Sarah. Even Tammy joined in by dragging a very reluctant Tucker into the dancing circle. Meanwhile, Gus, one of the whipsaw men began calling out dance steps:

Honor your partner!
Lady on the left!
Balance all!
All promenade!

Everyone was having a great time; especially Captain Bart and Ellen who danced every tune. Throughout the dancing, Joseph sat impassively next to Anna, who seemed to be enjoying the festivity as she nursed a hungry Little Fox.

Then, sadly, it was time for Tom Sutter and everyone accompanying him to return to the sawmill. As Tom and Sarah were saying goodbye to Millie, Jessie and the grandchildren, Captain Bart and Ellen stepped away from the group to be by themselves for little while. Tammy eyes followed every move they made, however, and when the two returned, Tammy went up to her aunt and whispered, "Aunt Ellen. Did Captain Bart just kiss you?" Ellen blushed and said, "Tammy Beckham, now you be minding your own business!"

However, Ellen's eyes were now on Captain Bart who was speaking with Jessie, Tom and Sarah. Moments later, Captain Bart came over to Ellen and Tammy with a big grin on his face. He gave Ellen a kiss on the cheek and then told everyone to stop what they were doing because he had an announcement.

96

"All right, everyone. Now listen up. That includes you scoundrels," he said to the crew of his barge. "Miss Ellen and I are going to be married!" Then he and Ellen hugged passionately amid the shouting, hooting and well-wishing from everyone. Without interrupting nursing Little Fox, Anna joined in the applause. Even Joseph smiled. Tammy jumped up and down while Tucker rolled his eyes. Captain Bart and Ellen had not known each other for very long – only a couple of months or so, actually. However, short courtships were not uncommon in Cracker country where there were very few eligible single people of either gender.

On a beautiful, clear day the following May, Captain Bart Robinson and Ellen Beckham were wed in the Episcopal church of Trinity Parish in St. Augustine. The wedding was attended by Jessie and Millie Beckham and their children, Millie's parents Tom and Sarah Sutter, several men from the sawmill and Captain Robinson's steam barge crew. It was a delightful and joyous occasion that all too soon would be marred by the dark clouds of secession that were beginning to form over Florida and the other southern states.

Chapter Thirteen

THERE WAS A SENSE OF GLOOM hanging over the group of legislators and dignitaries gathered at Florida Governor Madison S. Perry's plantation in Alachua County on the morning of November 9, 1860. Among those present were the outgoing Governor, himself, Governor-elect John Milton, Senator David Levy Yulee, Joseph Finnegan, John C. McGehee and several others. Awaiting results of the 1860 presidential election, the group's apprehension increased as an aide briskly walked up to the seated Governor and handed him a telegram just received from the State House in Tallahassee. Madison read the telegram, rose from behind his desk and solemnly spoke to those in the room.

"Gentlemen, it is terrible news. The results of the election held three days ago have now been tabulated. Lincoln won forty percent of the popular vote and handily beat the other three candidates: Breckenridge, Douglas and Bell." The room was filled with groans and curses. Madison raised his hands asking for quiet. Then, with great resolve he added, "I fear that our course of action has now been determined."

Immediately following the meeting at Governor Perry's plantation, the Florida legislature voted to hold an election to select delegates to a secession convention that would be held in the state's capitol in early January, 1861. Just three days before

Christmas in 1860, sixty-nine delegates were elected to attend the convention. On January 3, 1861, those delegates met in Tallahassee. Despite the pleading of a few anti-slavery advocates such as Judge William Marvin and Colonel W.C. Maloney in Key West, sixty-seven of the sixty-nine delegates voted for an ordinance of secession and for the organization of a confederacy of southern states. John C. McGehee, a longtime southern rights advocate, was elected permanent chairman of the convention.

Two days later, Senator David Yulee in Washington, D.C., telegraphed Joseph Finnegan, who was now in charge of all military affairs in the State of Florida, saying that "the immediately important thing to be done is the occupation of the forts and arsenals in Florida." Governor Perry (Governor-elect Milton would not be inaugurated until October 1861) ordered that the Florida Militia in St. Augustine take possession of Fort Marion, not a particular problem because the fort was manned by only one Union soldier, Ordinance Sergeant Henry Douglas.

It was early afternoon on a very cool day on January 7, 1861. Sergeant Douglas had just completed his scheduled afternoon inspection of the armaments along the fort's terreplein, the covered area between the inner and outer walls of the fort upon which cannons were positioned. Douglas cursed aloud at the stupidity of the Army that required daily inspections of weapons that were so old and outdated they likely could not even be fired safely. There was little risk that Sergeant Douglas' grumbling would be overheard. He was the only person – military or otherwise – who was in the fort, which for all practical purposes had been deactivated at the end of the Third Seminole War almost three years ago. Why the Army did not simply let the old antique crumble was beyond his understanding. On the other hand, it was great duty; there was no one left at the fort to bother him.

100

As Douglas began descending the ramp leading to the courtyard from the terreplein, he was surprised to see a squad of eight members of the Florida Blues Militia, a semi-military group, march into the fort through the sally port, it's only entrance, in the middle of the south curtain. The squad was led by a local named Clem Fulton, who was also a sometimes-drinking buddy of Sergeant Douglas. The Florida Blues Militia occasionally used the fort's courtyard to practice drills in a military setting rather than in the middle of the plaza in St. Augustine. When Sergeant Douglas reached the bottom of the ramp, Sergeant Fulton was waiting for him. His armed squad was standing at parade rest and a well-dressed civilian stood next to him.

"Hey there Clem. You guys planning to do some marching in here this afternoon?" Sergeant Douglas asked.

"Howdy Henry," Sergeant Fulton replied. "No, not today. Got some news for you, though," he said somewhat nervously. "Fraid you got to turn the fort over to us."

"What the hell! What do you mean turn it over to you?" Sergeant Douglas asked. "Did the Florida Blues buy it?"

"Not exactly, Henry," Sergeant Douglas said solemnly. "Governor Perry sent out an order for us to take possession of the fort immediately. Colonel Tarrington here is an aide-de-camp to Governor Perry and he can explain what this is all about."

Colonel Tarrington, a ranking officer in the Florida Blues Militia, though not in uniform, then informed Sergeant Douglas about the ordinance of secession and told him that the governor had ordered the militia to take possession of all union forts in the state as well as the armaments and magazines within them.

"Well, I'll be damned!" Sergeant Douglas exclaimed. "What the hell am I supposed to tell my commanding officer, Colonel Craig, in Washington?"

101

Both Tarrington and Fulton laughed. "Just tell him you put up a tremendous fight but that the boys in the militia got the best of you," Sergeant Fulton joked. "Look, Henry, there isn't much you can do about it. Why don't you just give us the keys to the fort and the magazine and then we'll all go back to town and have a drink at the tavern."

"Doesn't seem there is another choice," Sergeant Douglas said. "You have to give me a receipt for everything, though. And, you damn well better pay for the drinks!"

That done, the squad and the two sergeants and Colonel Tarrington, ambled back into town through the old city gates and headed for the St. George Tavern. Later, Sergeant Douglas wrote a brief report of the incident to his commanding officer, Colonel H. K. Craig, Chief of Ordinance Department, US Army:

SAINT AUGUSTINE, EAST FLORIDA

January 7, 1861

SIR:

I am obliged to perform what is to me a painful duty, viz, to report to the Chief of Ordnance that all the military stores at this place were seized this morning by the order of the governor of the State of Florida. A company of volunteer soldiers marched to the barracks and took possession of me, and demanded peaceable possession of the keys of the fort and magazine. I demanded them to show me their authority. An aide-de-camp of the governor showed me his letter of instructions authorizing him to seize the property, and directing him to use what force might be necessary.

Upon reflection, I decided that the only alternative for me was to deliver the keys, under protest, and demand a receipt for the property. One thing certain, with the exception of the guns composing the armament of the water battery, the property seized is of no great value. The gentleman acting under the governor's instructions has promised to receipt me for the stores.

I am, sir, very respectfully, your obedient servant,

Henry Douglas, Ordinance Sergeant, US Army

***

Millie missed Ellen's companionship very much. However, she and Ellen were able to visit each other often. When Ellen and Captain Bart married, he bought a homestead along the old Diego Road east of the sawmill where he built a small cedar plank house for the two of them. The Robinson home was barely two hours travel from the Beckham homestead. So, a social network of sorts soon developed between the Beckhams, Robinsons and Millie's parents Tom and Sarah Sutter. Of course, Tammy, now a young lady twelve years old, loved the occasions when she was allowed to stay at Aunt Ellen's house for a few days.

Tucker was sixteen years old. He was a tall, strong lad who his father badly needed to help work the farm, tap the pine trees and make turpentine. However, like other boys his age, Tucker had an adventurous spirit. Whenever he was not needed at the farm, such as during the winter season when farming activity came to a near stop and sap stopped running in the pine trees, Tucker would either go off by himself hunting in the swamp or forests or hitch a ride to St. Augustine on his uncle-by-marriage's barge. Actually, as time passed, Tucker became an able-bodied steam barge deckhand, himself.

It so happened that on one mild day in January, Tucker rode downriver on the steam barge to St. Augustine. After helping his uncle and the crew unload the barge's cargo, Tucker wandered up to the plaza where some sort of ruckus was going on near the Government House. There was a group of young men in civilian work clothes surrounding an Army colonel. The colonel was accompanied by a captain, who seemed to be his

103

aide, and a sergeant who had a musket slung over his shoulder. Other passersby stood back from the crowd around the colonel and were just observing the scene. Tucker walked up to one of the men observing the group and asked what the fuss was about.

"The colonel is a man named George Taliafero Ward," the man said. "He said he has been sent by Joe Finnegan, who is now a brigadier general, to recruit troops for the 2nd Florida Infantry stationed in Jacksonville."

"Why are they recruiting troops?" Tucker asked. "There is no war going on."

The man turned to Tucker and said, "Son, where the hell have you been? Don't you know that Florida, Mississippi and South Carolina have seceded from the Union and that other southern states are likely to follow right soon?"

"Seceded from the Union? What does that mean?" Tucker asked.

The man shook his head. "It means that as of a few days ago, Florida decided to tell the politicians in Washington, D.C. to pack their abolitionist garbage up their ass 'cause we don't need none of that crap down here," the man said. "We are an independent republic, now," he added. Then, he joined the enthusiastic applause of the crowd as three young men stepped up to stand next to the sergeant.

Tucker was still bewildered and was about to ask another question when he felt a hand on his left shoulder. He looked around to see Captain Bart standing next to him, chewing a plug of tobacco.

"There is no war yet, Tucker. However, I fear there is going to be one soon. Those young men have just enlisted in the Army of the newly formed Republic of Florida," the captain explained. "Come on, now. We best be getting back upriver," he added, spitting a stream of tobacco juice on the ground.

"Hey, you can't do that!" the man Tucker had been talking to exclaimed.

"Can't do what?" Captain Bart inquired.

"There is an ordinance here. You can't spit tobacco juice on the plaza ground."

Captain Bart pointed to a dog not far away who had his left leg raised and was "watering" a tree. "See that damn hound over there," Captain Bart asked the man.

"Yeah, what about it," the man curtly replied.

"Well sir," Captain Bart said. "If it's alright for that hound to piss on a tree, I figure it's alright for me to spit on the ground." With that, Captain Bart and Tucker left the scene and returned to the barge.

***

Florida seceded from the Union on January 10, 1861, breaking all ties with the United States of America and declaring itself a "sovereign and independent nation." However, its governmental structure remained unchanged. Then, less than one month later, on February 4, 1861, it was admitted to the confederacy, the Confederate States of America.

Chapter Fourteen

THE MOOD OF EVERYONE SEATED at the dinner table in the Robinson home was solemn. Ellen had invited Jessie, Millie and the children as well as Tom and Sarah Sutter to the Robinson home for a Sunday afternoon dinner. It was not a normal family social event, however. The family had gathered to discuss how they might respond to news that the Confederate Army had bombarded Fort Sumter in Charleston Harbor. Following the surrender of the fort, President Lincoln ordered that Union troops retake any federal forts that the Confederacy had captured, including those in Florida. Fort Marion, one of the forts taken by the Confederacy, was one of those Lincoln ordered retaken.

"My dear God," Jessie lamented. "This surely means war and we are in the middle of it."

Tom Sutter nodded his head in agreement. "It may be even worse than that," he said. "St. Johns County is divided. There are some who favor remaining in the Union while others are adamant that it was the correct decision to join the confederacy. In many ways, therefore, just like the country, itself, we are a people divided."

Tucker, who usually remained silent during family discussions, spoke. "I know that I am not yet seventeen years old. But, I will be soon. Like you, paw and you, mama, and like all of you, I am a southerner. I cannot imagine letting some northerner tell us what we can or cannot do." He turned to his father and said, "Paw, I want to join the Florida Blues Militia."

At his words, Millie and Ellen broke out in tears. Tammy did not fully understand the significance of what her brother said, but she took the clue from her mother and aunt and also began to weep, silently. The men at the table looked at Tucker with respect and shook their head. "Is this what it's all come to?" Tom Sutter asked. "Do we really want our brave young men like Tucker here to shed their blood for some stupid cause only the politicians understand?"

No one in the room spoke. The only sound was sniffles from the women. Jessie cleared his throat and replied to Tucker,

"Son, I know how you feel. However, just because there was a big ruckus in Charleston, it doesn't follow that there is any danger of fighting way down here in Florida." He reached over and patted Tucker on the arm. "Besides, spring is here and we have a lot of work to do tilling the fields and planting a new crop." Jessie's eyes were moist. "Your maw and I need you here, son."

Tucker lowered his head. "I know, paw. Still, I think I should join the militia just in case something happens here."

Jessie sighed. "Not yet, son. But, I know it might come to that someday. Remember, you are not seventeen yet and they would not let you join right now, anyway."

Tom Sutter changed the subject. "Bart, you get down river far more often than the rest of us. What about the fort and Lincoln's order that all Union forts captured by Southern troops be retaken by the Union Army?"

"Tom, I don't think we have any cause to be concerned about the Union Army coming this far south anytime soon.

However, what I hear is they might send the Navy to try to blockade ports like Jacksonville, Fernandina, St. Augustine, Tampa and Pensacola. Now that's a problem because except for a handful of Union frigates that were seized right after Sumter, the confederacy does not have a Navy to fight back and break a blockade."

"I don't understand. Why would they want to blockade St. Augustine?" Jessie asked. "It is not a deep sea port."

"Doesn't matter," Captain Bart said. "Even using just coastal packets we send a lot of foodstuff, lumber and marine stores like turpentine and rosin up north to Savannah and Charleston. The 'Yankees' will want to try to cut off those supplies."

"I wonder how serious a problem a blockade would really be," Tom Sutter mused. "Almost everybody here grows what they need for food, both crops and livestock. I don't see how they could starve us to surrender."

"It's not the foodstuff that's a problem," Captain Bart said. "We have most of the raw material we need to take care of ourselves. However, we have almost no manufacturing here. We need to bring in clothes, dry goods, medical supplies, coal, farm equipment and even powder and weapons from the north. That's where a blockade could hurt us."

Tears in her eyes, Millie asked, "Isn't there something we could do about all this?"

"Actually, there is," Captain Bart replied. "We know the estuaries and the inlets and they do not."

**

Captain Bart and his small crew, including Amos, Shane, Willie and, with the reluctant agreement of his parents, Tucker, steamed with the current of an ebbing tide down the Tolomato River to the public dock at St. Augustine. The only cargo on the ship was a few barrels of turpentine and rosin taken on at Cracker Landing and a few stacks of rough-cut planks from the sawmill - less than half the load the barge usually carried before the war. The barge arrived in the dark of night. After being quickly loaded with barrels of salted beef, pork, fish, fruit and salt destined for Confederate soldiers fighting in the Carolinas and Virginia, Captain Bart cast off and steered his barge south along the Matanzas River toward the inlet of the same name fifteen miles distant.

The barge carried no lights in order to avoid detection. Accurate navigation was crucial. Captain Bart ordered Shane forward to watch for obstacles and one man each on the port and starboard side of the barge. Shane also had the job of taking soundings to make sure the barge did not run aground. Willie made sure that the boiler's firebox was kept properly stoked. He was ready to provide maximum steam to the large piston turning the paddle wheel in the event Captain Bart ordered an increase in speed. All of the men, including Tucker (now seventeen) were armed with Model 1861 Springfield rifled muskets confiscated from the Fort Marion Armory when the Florida Blues Militia captured the fort a year earlier.

At 1:15 a.m., the barge passed the ruins of the old Fort Matanzas on its starboard side. Captain Bart slowed the vessel looking ahead for the prearranged signal that would indicate the "Dasher" had arrived and was waiting for them. Dasher was the name given blockade runners that slipped past Union ships stationed offshore, crossed the sandbar and took on contraband cargo from inland vessels like the steam barge. The transfer would have to be very quick because the Union Navy was constantly on the lookout for Dashers and their supply vessels. When the Navy spotted a Dasher, it would dispatch a squad of marines whose job it was to destroy the Dasher and its supply boat and kill or capture their crew.

110

"I see the lantern signal," Captain Bart said in a low voice. He had to be careful. Voices and other noise carried far at night, especially over the water. He lit a special lamp that had a three-inch square opening covered by a hinged tin flap. By opening and closing the flap in rapid succession, he returned the coded signal to the Dasher. A few minutes later, a longboat from the Dasher pulled alongside the barge and guided it to the anchored Dasher vessel, a coastal schooner. The crew of both vessels worked as quietly as possible transferring the barge's cargo to the schooner. At the same time, the captain of the schooner passed a leather bag filled with gold Liberty coins of various denominations to Captain Bart, who made certain that it contained the agreed upon payment.

When the transfers was done, Captain Bart turned his barge around so that it was heading north on the river and cast off the Dasher's schooner. However, Amos had no sooner thrown a line back to the schooner than shots rang out from the sand dunes just north of the inlet. The sky lit up by flares shot from the guns of a squad of Union marines, who were focusing their attention on the Dasher schooner now doing its best to escape through the inlet to open water.

"Hold your fire! They want the schooner – not us," Captain Bart shouted. "Willie give me as much steam as you can! We need to get the hell out of here!"

Willie turned the steam valve to its full open position and a surge of steam flooded into the cylinder forcing the piston to increase its strokes. Slowly, the paddle wheel increased the speed of its rotation and the barge began moving – at first at an agonizing crawl and then faster and faster. Suddenly, one or more of the marines noticed that the barge was trying to escape upriver and opened fire on it. Bullets thudded into the side of the barge as the crew crouched as low as they could under the starboard gunwale. The glass in the wheelhouse was blown out

111

by another round of shots from shore. At this point, Shane hollered, "Shit, fire back or the bastards will kill Bart!"

Tucker was frightened out of his wits. He was no stranger to rifles, muskets or even revolvers. Further, he was a good shot. However, he had never fired a weapon at another human being – never. But, as scared as he was, he also was no coward. So, along with Amos and Shane, Tucker raised himself up until he could see over the gunwale and with the others began firing. Amos shouted, "Aim at the flashes from their rifles!" Then, he howled in pain.

"Amos! Are you OK?" Captain Bart hollered.

"Yeah," Amos responded. "I got nicked in my right arm, though. Don't worry, I'm not bleeding too much and I can still fire back at them."

However, there was no need for further firing. By now, the barge had pulled far enough away that it was no longer a target for the marines on shore who were taking out their wrath on the Dasher schooner that was still struggling to get over the bar and pull away.

"Are they going to make it, captain?" Shane asked.

"I think so," Captain Bart said. "If they weren't they'd be on fire already." Then he called each man by name to make sure they were alright. Willie did not answer.

Shane ran to the stern of the barge to check on Willie and shouted out, "Oh my God, Captain. Willie's dead. He took a shot right in the middle of his chest."

It was first light when the barge tied up at the pier in St. Augustine. Amos, a bandage wrapped around his left arm, went to summon the harbormaster. A half-hour later, the harbormaster, accompanied by several volunteers from the Florida Blues Militia, climbed aboard the barge and removed Willie's body to a waiting wagon. While the militia carried

Willie's body off the barge, Captain Bart, Amos, Shane and Tucker stood at attention. There were tears in Captain Bart's eyes. Willie had been with him for over ten years. Captain Bart thought of Willie as a friend, not a slave. The barge would not be the same without him.

Afterwards, Tucker walked to the port side of the barge and stared at the lights of Fort Marion. Then, the tension and emotion of the day finally catching up to him, he shook violently and wretched over the side of the barge into the waters of the harbor. He had never seen a man die, before – especially a man with whom he had worked and fought. As he wiped his face with a wide handkerchief, he felt a hand on his shoulder. It was his uncle – his aunt's husband.

"Tucker, this has been a very difficult day for you – for all of us. One of our shipmates is dead, killed by the enemy. Let there be no mistake. You did your duty and you fought like the man you have become. We are truly at war now. It is sad for me to say, but there will surely be more deaths in the future. One thing is certain, however. Whatever Almighty God has in mind for you, I know you will do your duty bravely and competently. I would be proud to stand and fight alongside of you anywhere. Your parents have every right to be proud of you."

The next day, after the crew rested from the previous night's ordeal, Captain Bart ordered the steam barge to return to the sawmill. He briefly stopped at Cracker Landing, sounding the barge's whistle early enough that the entire Beckham family and Joseph and Anna were waiting for them at the landing pier. A stone-faced Tucker walked off the barge into the arms of his tearful mother. Captain Bart briefed Jessie about what had happened at Matanzas Inlet. Tammy hugged her older brother, not understanding what he had just been through. Jessie put his arm around Tucker's shoulder and they all walked up the path from the landing to the cabin as Captain Bart steered his barge away from Cracker Landing and back toward the sawmill.

Chapter Fifteen

LITTLE FOX WAS DELIGHTED to learn that in a few months he would have a little brother or sister. In the meanwhile, he was the star of the Beckham homestead. Jessie had persuaded Joseph that with another child on the way, the chickee was not the place for a family of four. So, when time permitted, he, Joseph and Tucker worked together replace the chickee with a small, single pen cabin.

While the men were busy trimming and notching cypress logs for the walls and floor of the new cabin, Anna and Little Fox were at the Beckham's cabin. Anna was helping Millie make a new patchwork quilt for the coming winter while Tammy repaired tears in some of the older quilts. Little Fox had the run of the cabin and enjoyed every minute of it. The women didn't worry about where he roamed because Stubby minded the three-year old as if he was his own pup. The twelve year-old hound took to that job readily because he felt somewhat displaced when Jessie acquired another, younger hunting dog. Fortunately, Stubby and the new dog, Maggie, got along quite well. The greater problem was that Tammy's cat Sissy and Maggie most certainly did not hit it off very well.

The two women and Tammy were sewing in silence when Anna spoke, "Miz Millie, Tucker does not say much these days."

Millie sighed. "Tucker has always been a quiet boy. However, yes, he has been more quiet than usual recently."

"Ever since Captain Bart ran the Union blockade and Willie got killed," Anna stated rhetorically.

"Yes, so I fear," Millie answered. "That was the first time Tucker ever shot a gun at anyone, or, for that matter, was ever shot at by someone. However, for certain, what affected him most was poor Willie getting killed."

"Tucker will be OK, Miz Millie. Don't you worry," Anna said. Then she suddenly stopped sewing as she placed a hand on her abdomen.

"Are you alright, Anna?" Millie asked in a worried voice.

"Yes ma'am. I just felt the baby kick. That was the first time he kicked!" she said excitedly.

"The first time "he" kicked," Millie repeated. "How do you know it will be a boy?"

"Little Fox needs a brother to grow up with and together learn all of the ways of our men. I can wait a while longer for a daughter."

Millie smiled. "Do you miss being with your people, Anna?"

"Yes ma'am," Anna replied. "But, we have a good life here. We are very grateful to you and Mizteh Beckham for all you have done for us."

"You have helped us a lot, too, Anna. Moreover, after Ellen got married and moved away, it has been somewhat lonely for me here at Cracker Landing. I am glad you are here. I enjoy the company of another woman."

The conversation between the two women was interrupted by the sound of a shotgun being fired coming from the direction of the cabin the men were building. Tammy exclaimed, "That is the sound of dinner, mama! Tucker must have shot something."

"That is probably true, Tammy, but why would it have to be Tucker who shot something?"

"Because Tucker is a better shot than paw," she said.

"Well, you better not let your paw hear you say that," Millie laughed.

Not much later, three very tired men, led by a brown and white mixed breed beagle, could be seen walking toward the cabin from the direction of the chickee. Maggie, who had stayed behind with the women, ambled down the cabin steps and sauntered out to meet the worn out construction crew with an air of indifference. Tammy noticed that both Tucker and Joseph were carrying wild turkeys - obviously trophies of their hunt.

"Mama, look!" Tammy said. "Tucker must have killed both turkeys with one shot. See! I told you he was a good shot," the proud younger sister exclaimed.

But then, Anna noticed that Joseph had his hunting bow slung over his shoulders. "He just wants to make sure he does not forget how to shoot straight," she quipped.

It was another couple of hours before dinner was ready. First, the women had to pluck and singe the turkeys which were then roasted on a spit over the outdoor fire pit. While the turkeys were roasting, they boiled turnips and made a loaf of fresh cornbread. It would be a fine meal this evening. Meanwhile, the men rested on the front porch. In order to help them relax better, Jessie broke open a new jug of Cracker Landing Lightning. However, as usual, Joseph did not imbibe, preferring plain, cool water instead. After Tucker's recent ordeal, Jessie felt his son had more than reached manhood and passed the jug to him. Tucker simply nodded to his father, held the jug over his right shoulder and took a full mouthful of the fiery liquid, violently spitting it out a moment later. "My gawd, paw! How can you drink that stuff?" he choked. Jessie laughed and was about to answer when a Union soldier with the rank of corporal accompanied by two privates carrying carbines unexpectedly marched up to the cabin.

***

Early in the Civil War, Confederate General Robert E. Lee ordered key Florida fortifications, including Fort Clinch in Fernandina and Fort Marion in St. Augustine to be reinforced. In St. Augustine, Fort Marion was manned by two companies of the Florida Militia, the Florida Blues commanded by Captain John Lott Philips and the Jefferson Beauregard's commanded by Captain Daniel E. Bird. However, in response to a shortage of troops needed in the central part of Florida and elsewhere, Lee later ordered that Fort Clinch be abandoned so that its troops could be repositioned.

Despite the strengthening of Confederate forces at Fort Marion, by early 1862 the Union blockade of St. Augustine was having a serious impact on the welfare of those who lived within the confines of the city. The major problem was lack of food supplies such as flour, rice, sugar, coffee, beef and pork. The situation was so dire that some of the poorer families had only enough food to provide one full meal per day. Those county residents who lived outside of the city and who owned a homestead with farmland had a much less severe experience since they grew their own crops and livestock.

Meanwhile, word began filtering in to St. Augustine that a Union naval fleet had left Fernandina and was en route south to capture New Smyrna where critical salt production facilities

were located. In response to this rumor, both companies of
Confederate soldiers located at Fort Marion were ordered south
to protect the more southern city. Accompanying the one
hundred troops of the "Blues" and "Jefferson's" were several
hundred St. Augustine men – many with their families – who
volunteered to fight for the Confederate cause. The end result
was that St. Augustine was left virtually undefended.
Unfortunately, the Union fleet was not headed for New Smyrna;
it was headed for St. Augustine.

On March 10, 1862, the USS Wabash, flagship of the
Southern Blockading Squadron, under the command of
Commodore Samuel F. DuPont dropped anchor off the coast of
St. Augustine, Florida. The Wabash was one of the most
powerful and intimidating warships of the line. Recognizing
that there was no alternative except surrender, Acting St.
Augustine Mayor Christobal Bravo signaled the city's surrender
by flag and indicated there would be no resistance to any Union
troops taking possession of the city. The next day, Commander
C. R. P Rodgers and a small contingent of marines under the
command of Captain Daniels landed at the city pier and raised
the Union flag over Fort Marion. They could not raise the Union
flag over the St. Francis Barracks at the south gate of the city
because a small group of ladies had chopped down the flagpole
to prevent that event.

***

Millie and Anna were working under the shade of the
outdoor kitchen's thatched roof when the Union soldiers
marched up to the cabin. Tammy was stirring the turnips being
boiled in the pot hung over a hot fire. Everyone in the
Beckham's extended household stared in shock and
bewilderment at the sight before them. Jessie and Tucker had an
instinctive impulse to grab their rifles. However, that thought
passed immediately as they realized that such action, in addition

119

to being basically foolish, would jeopardize the safety of the women.

The corporal leading the small contingent smartly saluted the Beckhams and politely said, "Good afternoon, ladies and gentlemen. I am Corporal Greg Latham, United States Marines, 4th New Hampshire Regulars. Please accept my apologies for the intrusion."

The corporal could see the look of shock and disbelief on the faces of everyone. He continued, "Perhaps you have not yet heard the news; however, two days ago Acting Mayor Cristobal Bravo surrendered the city of St. Augustine to Commander Rodgers, Commanding Officer of the armed frigate USS Wabash, who accepted it on behalf of Commodore DuPont, Commanding Officer of the Southern Atlantic Blockading Squadron. The Union flag now flies again over Fort Marion and the City of St. Augustine."

Jessie spoke up first, "How did you get here?"

"By boat – a Union blockade gunboat, actually. Am I correct that this is what the folks in town call Cracker Landing?"

Jessie simply nodded. Then Corporal Latham told them about the events of the past several days. He emphasized that everything transpired in a peaceful and respectful way, except that there was a group of ladies in town who seem to take pleasure in harassing Union troops whenever they came upon any. Millie put a hand to her face to cover a smile of approval. Then the corporal turned to more serious matters.

"If you forgive me," he said respectfully. "I have been ordered to ask you a few questions." Without waiting for a reply, he continued. "Has anyone here sheltered Confederate troops or participated in any activities to counter the Union blockade of St. Augustine?"

Jessie and Millie quietly inhaled deeply thinking about Tucker and Captain Bart. However, Tucker simply continued to look at the marine corporal impassively. They all shook their heads to indicate "no."

"Well, that's good," Corporal Latham said. "A couple of weeks ago there was a blockade running attempt way down at Matanzas Inlet. That was an illegal activity. More important, one of our marines was killed in action and two others were wounded. I don't suppose any of you know anything about that incident, do you?"

Again, everyone shook their head in the negative. This was the first time, however, that they heard anything about Union soldiers being killed or wounded. Tucker wondered if those casualties were the result of any shots fired from the steam barge. He had observed that the heaviest exchange of fire was between the soldiers on shore and those on the dasher's schooner.

"I am surprised to see those two Seminole Indians here with you," Corporal Latham said. "Why are they here? Are they runaways?"

"They work the farm for me," Jessie said. "Anything wrong with that?"

"No sir, nothing at all. Just wondered," the corporal replied. "Except, seems that there are hardly any Indians left here in the county. Almost all of them have fled into the Ocala or father south."

Anna and Joseph had a blank look on their faces seemingly ignoring the corporal's comments. Then, Corporal Latham said that Acting Mayor Bravo had been given permission to continue to run the city government just as before without interference from the Union authorities, as long as everything remained peaceful and there was no further insurrection activity against the United States of America.

121

However, when he mentioned that his next stop was the sawmill, Jessie and Millie thought their hearts would stop. They both knew that the incident at Matanzas Inlet the corporal mentioned earlier involved Captain Bart and crew, including Tucker. For his part, Tucker just glared at the corporal, who was probably only a year or two older than him.

Once again, the corporal apologized for intruding on the Beckhams. He saluted and, together with the three privates, smartly wheeled around and marched back toward the landing. Jessie and Millie were visibly relieved when they left. Tammy asked her mother what that was all about. Joseph and Anna sat as they had been, expressionless. However, Tucker whispered something to Joseph and before Jessie could even ask a question, Tucker ran into the cabin, grabbed two rifles, throwing one to Joseph, and the two took off like greased lightning toward the swamp. There was just enough time before the two disappeared for Millie to shout "Tucker! Please be careful!"

***

Tucker had no intention of getting into a losing battle with the United States Marines. He simply wanted to see the Union gunboat. Wisely, Tucker always carried a weapon when going into the swamp. The two men followed a path well known to them that cut through an alternating combination of shallow water and dry hammocks. At the end of the path was one of Tucker's favorite fishing spots, an inlet from the river that was completely hidden from view by dense foliage. The two men squatted down among the scrub palmettos and waited. It was not long until the gunboat came into view.

Tucker was astounded. His impression was that the gunboat was sleek and fast. It must have been traveling at six or seven knots or even more, leaving a wake that crashed into the riverbank as it sped along. He recognized that it must be screw-driven because it lacked a paddle wheel. Although it was

122

powered by steam like a paddle wheel boat, the propulsion gear for a screw-driven vessel was below deck; therefore, it produced less noise than a paddle wheeler. The gunboat was not large, probably less that seventy-feet in overall length. However, it was heavily armed. Tucker could see several small naval guns, perhaps four pounders, on both the port and starboard sides of the vessel. He could also see at least a dozen seamen and marines at various stations as the boat passed within less than twenty yards of where he and Joseph were watching.

When the boat passed, Tucker spat on the ground in contempt of what he saw. He tried to stifle the anger and frustration within him. He was very concerned that there was no way he could warn Captain Bart, his aunt and grandparents that Union marines were on their way to the sawmill. Worse yet, he could not warn Captain Bart that the marines were looking for anyone who participated in running the blockade.

Chapter Sixteen

Amos PEABODY WAS GUIDING a two-inch hawser through a cathole in the bow of the steam barge when he looked up and saw the Union gunship approaching the sawmill pier. He stood up, dropped the hawser on the deck of the barge and watched as the Union vessel drew closer. A sailor on the gunboat hailed him and said that the gunboat would drop anchor a ship's length downriver and would then send over a boarding party to inspect the barge. Amos shouted something to Shane who leaped off the barge and went to fetch Captain Bart.

By the time the boarding party's longboat reached the barge, Captain Bart was already aboard. A sailor from the longboat threw a line to Shane and soon the Union crew of four sailors led by a young ensign climbed over the gunwale of the barge. The Union seamen were armed only with side arms which were all holstered. There was no need for other weapons; the armament on the gunboat would deter anything but determined resistance by anyone on shore or on the barge.

The young naval officer saluted casually and introduced himself as Ensign Robert Caldwell, commanding officer of the United States gunboat *Pequot*. Captain Bart introduced himself and his crew and asked by what authority the ensign had boarded his vessel. Ensign Caldwell asked if Captain Bart or any member of his crew knew that St. Augustine had been recaptured by the United States Navy. Captain Bart said no, which was a lie.

In fact, a few hours earlier, one of the merchants in St. Augustine who did business with the sawmill sent a messenger by horseback to the mill to warn them a Union gunboat was headed upriver. Unlike the Beckham homestead that was miles away from any road leading to St. Augustine, the sawmill was near the old Pablo Road that connected the city with fortified positions along the St. Johns River. When the messenger arrived, Tom Sutter, foreman of the mill, gathered all of the mill's workers together and briefed them on what had happened in St. Augustine. Then he ordered them to help Captain Bart repair or at least hide the damage the barge suffered during the skirmish at Matanzas Inlet.

Responding to Captain Bart's question, Ensign Caldwell said, "By the authority of Commander C. R. P Rodgers, United States Navy, sir. Commander Rodgers accepted the surrender of St. Augustine from acting Mayor Bravo this past Monday."

"I see," Captain Bart said. "What do you want here, Ensign?"

"We are looking for a vessel that was involved in a blockade running operation at Matanzas Inlet, recently. We plan on inspecting this steam barge to see if it was that vessel."

"And, if you find what you are looking for...what then?"

"Then we confiscate the vessel and arrest the crew. We lost one man and two were injured in the firefight that took place when we were trying to apprehend the dashers," Ensign Caldwell said.

"Sorry to hear about the casualties," Captain Bart said. "Did you capture the dashers?"

"No, their schooner slipped through our blockade. The vessel we are looking for, however, was reported to sail north in the Matanzas River. So, it is very likely an inland water vessel – like a steam barge, for example."

Ensign Caldwell was interrupted when one of his sailors came up to him. "Ensign," the man said. "You might want to look at what we found."

Ensign Caldwell followed the seaman to the port gunwale of the barge where another seaman was leaning over the railing digging into a small hole that had been filled with a hard substance that the Ensign identified as a mixture of rosin and sawdust.

"Hey! What are you doing making a hole in the gunwale?" Captain Bart shouted.

Ensign Caldwell looked up. "Those holes are just about the size of a 58-caliber musket ball. Maybe we'll find one inside the hole. If so, then you folks have some explaining to do."

"That's ridiculous!" Captain Bart exclaimed. "Those aren't from musket balls! We get those holes all the time from the carpenter bees around here. The little critters make perfectly round holes about a half-inch in diameter with their sharp teeth. Then they crawl inside and lay eggs. The only way to get rid of them is to patch their holes with rosin."

"Look, sir. There are several more of them!" Another sailor pointed to patched holes along the outside of the gunwale.

"Captain Bart, I find your explanation implausible," Ensign Caldwell said.

It looked very much like the ensign was about to confiscate the barge and arrest its crew. Then, Tom Sutter arrived. He climbed aboard the barge and spoke to the young naval officer. "Son," he said somewhat patronizingly, "I am

Tom Sutter, the foreman of this mill. I'd like to ask where you are from."

"Connecticut. Why do you ask, sir?"

"Ever seen gators or wild hogs or even palm trees before?"

"Can't say I have, Mr. Sutter. However, what does that have to do with these holes that sure look like they have been made when a 58-caliber ball hit them?"

"Well, maybe you haven't seen southern carpenter bees in action, either," Sutter replied. "Mind taking a short walk with me. Just over there to the cookhouse."

Ensign Caldwell instructed his men to remain where they were. Tensions were high and it was clear that something very unpleasant might happen at any moment. Unseen by the gunboat crew, Tom Sutter had positioned several of his sawmill workers in the brush and trees surrounding the mill and pier. Others were in the bunkhouse and sawmill pits – all armed with rifled Springfield's and Enfield's aimed at the exposed crew of the gunboat. Sutter had been a cavalry captain during the Seminole wars. Several of his men were veterans, also. They knew how to fight in combat. Still, Sutter knew he and his men would be no match for the four-pounder naval guns mounted on the gunboat.

Sutter and Caldwell walked over to a section of the cookhouse where the fascia under the eaves of the roof had several round holes the size of a musket ball patched with a rosin and sawdust mix. Sutter called one of his workers over to join them. "This is Pappy Smith," Sutter said. "Pappy, pop one of those patches for us."

As the ensign looked on, Pappy began prying the rosin from one of the holes. When the plug was free, he removed it and Sutter stuck his finger in the hole. When he withdrew his finger, it was covered with a thick amber substance. Sutter licked the amber material from his finger and asked Pappy to pry the rosin out of another hole. That done, he told the ensign to put his finger in the hole. The young officer hesitated then carefully inserted the tip of his finger in the hole. When he withdrew his finger, it, too, was covered with the same amber material. "Taste it," Sutter said.

"I'll be damned!" Ensign Caldwell exclaimed. "It's honey."

"And bees make honey. That's what we've been telling you, young man," Sutter said. "Now, would you like to see the rest of the mill?"

"No, sir," Ensign Caldwell replied. "Sorry to have bothered you."

"No bother at all, I assure you," Sutter replied.

The two men walked back to the pier where Ensign Caldwell told his men to get back onboard the gunboat. Ten minutes later, the gunboat hauled in its anchor and headed downriver back toward St. Augustine. When it was out of sight, all of the sawmill workers and barge crew drew a big sigh of relief.

"What the hell did you tell him?" Captain Bart asked Tom Sutter. "I thought for sure we'd be in a shooting match by now."

"I didn't actually tell him anything," Sutter said. "I just asked Pappy to pop a couple of the holes he drilled in the fascia board a couple of hours ago. When Pappy drilled the holes, I told him to stuff some honey in them and plug the holes with rosin just like the ones on the gunwale of your barge. I knew damn well that someone would spot those musket ball holes. Lucky you pried the balls out of the holes before you patched them. If Caldwell found one we'd all be up to our ass in blood right now."

Sutter paused for a minute and then said, "Bart, you did have your men pry out the musket balls, didn't you?"

Captain Bart looked at Shane and then walked over to the patch that the Navy seaman had been ready to pry out. He asked for Shane's knife, pried the rosin out of the hole and looked inside. A lead 58-caliber musket ball stared at him. Feeling queasy, Captain Bart handed Shane the knife and walked away without answering Sutter's question.

***

The scruffy bearded man riding an emaciated looking pony down St. George Street toward the city's north gate was indistinguishable from any other Florida Cracker passing through St. Augustine. His soiled dark blue canvas trousers were supported by frayed suspenders. The grey long-sleeve rough cotton shirt he wore was long overdue for a wash. His soiled and crumpled broad-brim felt hat and muddy calf-high leather boots suggested that he had either been herding cattle or tilling a field. It was probably herding cattle because in addition to the Cracker pony, a tough looking black cur dog walked by his side. Everybody knew that Cracker cowboys used cur dogs to herd ornery scrub cows that grazed in the vast open range west of the St. Johns River. When he passed by a Union soldier, he gave the thumbs up sign or a half-salute, which they often returned. In other words, he fit in perfectly with many of the other Crackers walking through the city's streets – at least those sympathetic to the Union.

The two Union privates guarding the north gate of the ancient city were bored. Bored and hot. They had been on duty for over two hours and it would be still another two hours before they were relieved by the next watch. For the past two hours, their only activity had been to wave on a few dozen locals who passed through the gate either on foot or horseback. A handful of farmers and merchants had driven wagons through the gate as well. However, unlike the foot and horseback travelers, the wagons were searched to make sure they were not carrying contraband goods that would aid the enemy – the Army of the Confederate States of America that held much of the territory north and west of St. Augustine.

Captain John Jackson Dickinson, Commanding Officer of Company H, 2nd Florida Cavalry, Confederate States of America casually prodded the Cracker pony and his borrowed cur dog up to the two Union soldiers standing in the shadow of the coquina framed city gate. Dickinson had been through this routine several times before. On this day, his mission was completed. Dressed in the garb of a typical Cracker Cowboy, Dickinson had spent the day reconnoitering the fortifications of the city from one end to the other, including the harbor and its defenses. He had determined the strength of the Union forces occupying the city, the armament they could bring to bear and the morale and combat readiness of the troops. Now he was ready to leave the city and return to the cavalry company he commanded that was waiting for him across the St. Johns River opposite Tocoi, seventeen miles west.

Dickinson dismounted the pony and ambled up to the guards. In a practiced Cracker accent, he greeted them saying simply, "Howdy gents." The guards smiled and returned his greeting. Then, determined to squeeze the last morsel of intelligence information from his venture into the city, he spat out a long stream of tobacco juice and the wad he had been chewing and added, "Bah, damn stuff got stale." He reached into his back pocket and pulled out a twist of homegrown chewing tobacco. He broke off one piece for himself and offered the twist to the two guards asking, "You gents want a chew?" They both gratefully accepted a piece of the twist as Dickinson tore off a generous wad for each man. Then he began his interrogation.

"I hear Colonel Bell is pissed because he can't get the supplies he needs to beef up the garrison," he said. Dickinson was referring to Colonel Louis Bell, 4th New Hampshire Volunteers, who was the first commander of the St. Augustine post after its surrender to Commander Rodgers.

"Ha, that's the least of it," the first guard replied. "I hear that there is a real muck up with canister shot being sent for the new sixteen inch naval guns and solid rounds for the howitzers."

"That's right!" the second guard laughed. "So, the idiots in the ordnance department sent the Colonel anti-personnel shot for bombarding ships at sea and solid round shot for the howitzers used for any enemy attacking the fort or town. Just the opposite of what was needed!"

"I'll tell you what really pisses off old Bell," the first guard offered. "It's that he can't catch that rebel cavalry captain they call the War Eagle."

"Who is the War Eagle?" Dickinson asked, doing his best to keep a straight face.

"It's some rebel company commander who has been playing hell with our supply wagons and patrols," the second guard said. "He keeps showing up where you might least expect him and then the first thing you know, he and his cavalry and sharpshooters have just killed or captured a whole squad or platoon."

"He even has made raids right here under the nose of the cannons of the fort," the first guard added. "It's so bad that at night anyone wearing a Union uniform had better be sleeping inside the fort or aboard the Wabash. Otherwise he's liable to wake up with a rebel pistol pointed at his head."

Dickinson shook his head and grunted. "Seems like one clever guy to me. No wonder Colonel Bell is so upset." Then, having gathered enough additional intelligence information, he jovially waved to the two guards and passed through the ancient city's gate. An hour later, Dickinson guided his pony along an old farm road that ended at an abandoned homestead. Waiting for him in the dilapidated Cracker house were a sergeant and two privates.

After changing into a Confederate Cavalry Officer's uniform and exchanging the Cracker pony for a sprightly cavalry horse, Dickinson and his party galloped off to Tocoi, a crossing point on the St. Johns River, where a ferry waited for them. Another hour later, he was reunited with the men of his company and they set off for Company H's campsite upriver. The "War Eagle," as Dickinson had become known to the men of the 2nd CSA Cavalry had much work to do. Also known to Colonel Bell and the occupying Union forces as "Dixie," the "War Eagle began to prepare for his next raid on Union forces.

Later, in his tent at the company's campsite, Captain Dickinson and Lieutenants McCardell and McEaddy reviewed a map of the region that encompassed an area east and south of the St. John's River. Dickinson studied the map carefully and then spotted the site he was searching. It was an old Spanish colonial era fortification called Fort Diego, the former homestead of Don Diego Espinosa who once owned 60,000 acres of grazing and farming land in the mid eighteenth century. The Spanish governor of La Florida, as the state was called at the time, authorized Don Diego to build a palisade fort surrounding his hacienda as a defense against both marauding Indians and the invading English under the command of British General James Oglethorpe. Ultimately, the fort was captured by the British. However, the fort was abandoned some twenty years later and now lay in ruins.

What Dickinson learned while gathering intelligence information in St. Augustine, however, was that Union patrols regularly bivouacked on the site because it offered them a clear range of fire and was easily protected from any enemy, whether Indians, marauders or Confederates soldiers. In particular, he learned that Colonel Bell's adjutant, Major Schneller, several junior officers and a contingent of fifty-to sixty men were planning to be there the following Saturday.

After consulting with his two subordinates, the War Eagle circled the site with a pen. Next, he plotted a route that would take him and a contingent of his men close to that location, avoiding any of the main roads patrolled by Union soldiers. The route would take Dickinson back across the St. Johns River at Tocoi and then east through open range and farm roads to just south of Durbin Swamp. From there they would continue further east until they arrived at the smaller Diego swamp. That would give them a safe, backwoods path to a point south of old Fort Diego. Dickinson, McCardell and McEaddy agreed, however, that before they made a direct attack on the Union forces camped there, though, they would need a good staging area for their troops.

Scanning the map again, Dickinson spotted the ideal place – it was sufficiently secluded that it would not likely come under observation by Union troops. Further, it was strategically located where it could provide easy access and egress to and from the Union's bivouac location. Dickinson circled that site and informed his lieutenants that they would mount up and leave for the staging location at first light.

Chapter Seventeen

It WAS A LAZY, PEACEFUL DAY. As usual, most of the Beckhams arose from bed at dawn, which at this time of year was about 6:35 a.m. A couple hundred yards from the Beckham cabin, however, Joseph and Anna were already busy with daily chores. Anna made a breakfast gruel of corn meal for herself, Joseph and Little Fox while she nursed her beautiful newborn daughter who they had named Little Flower. As soon as he finished breakfast, Joseph left their one-room cabin to milk the cow and goats. Meanwhile, Anna took the children up to the main cabin to help Millie prepare breakfast for the Beckhams.

Jessie rolled out of bed and noticed that Millie had risen before him – as usual. He slipped into his trousers, went over to the porcelain washbasin on the stand next to the unused chamber pot, poured cold water in the basin from the pitcher and washed his face with his hands. He dried his face on a cotton towel Millie made a year ago. Then he put on a rough weave cotton shirt and pulled his suspenders over the shirt. He once tried using a belt to hold up his trousers. However, as Millie often pointed out, his hips were the wrong shape and without suspenders, his trousers would soon be bunched on the floor at his feet. Running his fingers through his unkempt hair, Jessie looked at himself in the only mirror in the room. With mild concern, he noted that there was more grey hair on his head than there used to be. Not much I can do about that, he thought. He was more displeased by the straggly look of his grey speckled beard. "I'll have to borrow Millie's scissors and trim that back a bit," he thought. Then, he shrugged and walked out of the cabin onto the wrap-around porch.

The sound of mourning doves searching for fallen grain in the cornfields greeted him as he walked to the porch railing. It would still be another quarter hour before the sun rose above the horizon. However, the dawn's light was sufficient to enable the homestead work routine to begin. As he had guessed, Millie and Anna were already beginning to prepare breakfast. A large coffee pot sat on the cast iron grate that covered much of the outdoor kitchen's fire pit. He savored the aroma of the coffee and wondered how much longer he would be able to enjoy it. Coffee was only one of the commodities that were in scarce supply because of the war. Sadly, although the farm was mostly self-sufficient, coffee, salt and a few other foodstuffs had to be purchased from other sources.

Tammy came bouncing out of the cabin. She went over to her father and gave him a big kiss. Jessie asked if she slept well. She said that she did until Tucker started to snore loudly. Tucker, who was the last of the family to arise, came out on to the porch just in time to hear his sister's complaint. He called her a crybaby and a fusspot and told her to stop complaining – especially first thing in the morning. Tammy stuck her tongue out at Tucker and ran down the porch steps to see if she could help her mother. Meanwhile, Joseph came up to the house from the barn carrying a pail of fresh milk in one hand and a basket of a half-dozen eggs in the other.

"Paw, what do we have to do this morning?" Tucker asked his father.

"Not much, I guess. What do you have in mind?"

136

"Well sir, I propose that you, me and Joseph go hunting after breakfast and see if we can bag a duck or two. Then, this afternoon, after doing whatever chores might be lined up, I want to see if I can land a couple of redfish. They're running right about now."

"Sounds good to me," Jessie said. "What do you think, Joseph?" Rather than a formal reply, Joseph simply gave a thumbs up sign and nodded his head.

Shortly after sunrise, they all enjoyed a breakfast of salt pork fried in tallow, hominy, cornbread, coffee sweetened with fresh milk and sugar and freshly picked oranges from the orange trees Millie planted after the hurricane. Then, the three men slung shot pouches over their shoulders and headed off to Diego Swamp to hunt ducks. Their smoothbore muskets were primed to fire rounds of buckshot for this trek.

***

Diego Swamp lay to the east of its larger cousin Durbin Swamp. Geologically, at some distant time in the past both swamps might have been connected. Despite the disparity of their size – Durbin Swamp was several times larger than Diego Swamp – they both shared the same characteristics as most any swamp in the northern part of Florida: shallow water usually only a foot or two deep alternating with dry hammocks. This means that in most cases the swamp can be navigated on foot. However, there is one important difference between the two swamps. Durbin Swamp is spring fed while Diego Swamp is fed by tidal water flowing in from a creek linked to the brackish Tolomato River. In fact, Diego Swamp runs right into a salt marsh estuary off the Tolomato River making it an ideal place to find resting Mallards or Black-Bellied Whistling Ducks.

Jessie, Tucker and Joseph knew Diego Swamp as though it was their private hunting preserve. They had hunted in the swamp many times and knew where every path and turn would

137

lead. Still, the swamp was filled with danger such as Diamond Back Rattlesnakes, Water Moccasins, sharply tusked wild boars, alligators, quicksand and other hazards. However, all three men had hunted in swamps most of their lives, so they were well aware of the possible dangers and carefully avoided them.

Using hand signals in order to avoid making any kind of noise that would spook their prey, the three men approached a spot where the swamp merged with the salt marsh. Just as Tucker had expected, ahead of them was a flock of a dozen or so Mallards floating peacefully on the brackish water, occasionally dipping their heads under water as they foraged for tender plants. They began priming and loading their muskets when Joseph's senses told him something was wrong. He held up his hand.

"What's wrong, Joseph?" Jessie asked.

Joseph put his finger to his lips for quiet. Then he whispered, "Listen."

"I don't hear anything," Tucker said.

"Neither do I," said Jessie.

"That's the problem," Joseph replied. "Where is the noise of the birds or the sound of a coot or a squirrel? I don't even hear the sound of a rabbit or a raccoon or even a rat rustling through the brush."

"You are right," Jessie said with obvious concern. "The swamp is too quiet. Also, look at the Mallards. They are slowly but surely moving together out into open water."

Jessie had barely stopped speaking when in mass, the Mallards began flapping their wings, quacking and then they took off – frightened by something. Simultaneously, a voice was heard coming from only a few yards behind the three men.

"Sorry to spook the Mallards, gentlemen. However, we need your help."

Jessie, Tucker and Joseph turned in unison. A man no older than Tucker wearing a grey uniform and a Confederate forage cap walked out of the shadows. He was carrying a Springfield 1861 musket. A chevron of sergeant stripes were sewn on his sleeves. Accompanying him were five Confederate soldiers, all in Confederate greys and all carrying either Springfield muskets or Burnside carbines.

"I am Sergeant Charles Dickinson, Company H, 2nd Florida Cavalry, CSA. My father is Captain John J. Dickinson, commanding officer of this company. He is called the War Eagle. You might have heard of him."

Jessie, Tucker and Joseph were flabbergasted. They simply nodded and made sure that their muskets were lowered. Finally, Jessie spoke. "What do you want from us sergeant?"

"Nothing too much," the young sergeant said. "We just want to borrow Cracker Landing for a day or so."

***

It was early in the afternoon when Jessie, Tucker and Joseph returned to the Beckham homestead under the watchful eyes of Sergeant Dickinson and his men. Jessie was staggered by the sight he saw as he approached the cabin. Two dozen tethered cavalry horses and several pack mules were grazing near the barn. Several Confederate soldiers lounged in the area in front of the cabin playing cards and chewing tobacco. Seated on the porch next to Millie were the War Eagle, himself, and another officer who was later introduced as Lieutenant McEaddy. Both men were smoking cigars. When Jessie climbed the stairs, Captain Dickinson stood up, offered his hand, which Jessie readily shook, and introduced himself and Lieutenant McEaddy.

139

"I truly apologize for the inconvenience and intrusion," Captain Dickinson said. "However, we are here on an important mission and require your assistance and cooperation for a little while."

"What is it that you need specifically, Captain?" Jessie asked.

The War Eagle told Jessie that he and his men were preparing to engage Union forces in a skirmish some miles from Cracker Landing. He said that for security purposes he could not discuss the details of the engagement. However, he said that until they were ready for the skirmish, he needed a place for his men to rest and prepare for action. Would it be alright if they made temporary camp here on the Beckham homestead?

Jessie looked at Millie who clearly was as perplexed as he was. "What do you think, Millie?" Jessie asked.

"The captain and his men have been very courteous and kind," she replied. "In fact, while we were waiting for you to return, he gave us some supplies we have had trouble getting." She pointed to several sacks lined up on the porch clearly marked *Sugar, Salt, Coffee* and *Flour*.

"Good heavens, Captain. That is most generous of you!" Jessie exclaimed.

"In a way, you can thank the Yankees for them," Dickinson said with a smile. "We captured those supplies and a lot more during some of our raids. However, back to the matter at hand. What do you say, Mr. Beckham? May we stay here a few days?"

Jessie knew that Dickinson was being gratuitous. He could easily have simply commandeered the homestead for as long as he wanted. There would be nothing Jessie could do about it, anyway.

Before Jessie could respond, Tucker spoke. "Paw, Captain Dickinson and his men are fighting for you, me, mama and everyone here in Florida. We have to do our part."

Millie nodded in agreement. As usual, Joseph and Anna remained expressionless. Tammy was not paying a bit of attention to what was being said. She was busy flirting with the captain's son.

"Of course, captain," Jessie replied. "We would be honored to have you and your men remain here for as long as you need."

Dickinson beamed. "It's settled then. I suggest that we encamp at the far end of your crop field toward that small cabin," he pointed toward Joseph's and Anna's cabin near the southern boundary of Diego Swamp. "I assure you that my men are well disciplined and will cause you no problem. Meanwhile, I have posted two men down at your pier to keep a lookout for anyone, military or civilian, who might be passing by on the river or planning to stop at Cracker Landing."

Jessie agreed that would be a good idea. Although not completely out of sight from the main cabin, it would be easy for the Confederate soldiers to disappear into the heavily wooded area bordering the field or into the swamp, if needed. Dickinson gave a nod to Lieutenant McEaddy who, in turn, ordered Sergeant Dickinson to round up the men and move them to the end of the homestead property. Then, Dickinson said he and Lieutenant McEaddy wanted some information that he thought Jessie and Tucker might be able to supply. Jessie went into the cabin for a moment, returning with a jug of Cracker Landing Lightning and four tin cups. Nodding in approval, the War Eagle got down to business.

"I need to make contact with a man I believe you know. His name is Captain Bart Robinson."

141

Jessie and Tucker were surprised. How much did this man know about them and their family, they wondered.

Dickinson continued, "I can tell by the expression on your faces that you both wonder how I know about Captain Robinson. I can tell you that I am aware that Captain Bart, as you call him, is fully sympathetic to our cause and has already performed a valuable service to it – and that includes you, Tucker."

"You know about us running the blockade, then," Tucker said.

"Yes, that and more," Dickinson said. He chose not to reveal how much intelligence information he picked up while roaming freely around St. Augustine. "The point is that I need Captain Bart's barge. Can you make contact with him for me, Tucker?"

"Yes sir, I certainly can," Tucker proudly responded. He felt honored and excited to be part of the War Eagle's plans, whatever they were.

"Good," Dickinson replied. "In that case, as soon as Sergeant Dickinson returns, I want you to accompany him to the sawmill and contact Captain Bart. Sergeant Dickinson will take over after you make contact," he said.

At that point, Dickinson relaxed and poured himself a hefty portion out of the jug Jessie offered him. He took a long drink of the fiery liquid and said, "Damn, that's fine liquor!"

Chapter Eighteen

CAPTAIN BART PEERED AHEAD trying to make out the outline of Cracker Landing's pier in the weak predawn light. In the dark of night, he had inched the barge along, guided by Shane on the starboard bow and Amos on the port bow. For the past hour, they had been using their lanterns to signal whether he should steer to port or starboard to remain in the middle of the river and away from its muddy banks. Finally, he could make out the pier about a quarter mile ahead.

There would be no sounding of the barge's steam whistle today. The sound of steam being released after each stroke of the single large piston and the clatter of the paddle wheel made enough noise, interrupting the morning quiet. On this mission, Captain Bart did not want to alert the entire countryside that he was approaching Cracker Landing. Besides, the lookouts posted on the pier would have already spotted the barge and informed the War Eagle that it was arriving.

A few minutes later, the barge glided up to the landing and lines were tossed to Jessie and Joseph, who quickly secured them to the pier's pilings. Lastly, the spring line was fastened to the large cleat bolted to the deck of the pier. Moments later, Captain Bart, Tucker, Sergeant Dickinson and the soldiers accompanying him debarked the barge. Amos, Shane and the new boiler man who replaced Willie, a strong Negro named

Henry, remained aboard. Then, the men who had debarked the barge walked up the path to the cabin where Captain Dickinson and Lieutenant McEaddy were waiting.

Sergeant Dickinson stood at attention and crisply saluted his father, who returned the young man's salute complimenting him on a job well done. He also thanked Tucker for his help and introduced himself and the lieutenant to Captain Bart.

"I take it that Sergeant Dickinson has briefed you on what we plan to do next," the War Eagle said to Captain Bart. Sergeant Dickinson had informed Captain Bart that his father needed the barge to transport cavalry horses and soldiers to the sawmill where they would debark. From there, the cavalry contingent would proceed on land to a location where they would engage the enemy. Once they left the sawmill, they would have no further need to use the barge – unless the unforeseen happened and they needed another escape route.

"I have, sir," Captain Bart replied. "The deck of the barge is clear. However, it's going to be very tight if we take all two dozen of your horses and their riders aboard at the same time."

"It will be eighteen – not two dozen," Captain Dickinson said. "Corporal Toby Piggot and five other men will take the pack animals and rendezvous with us at another location."

"Then, there will be no problem, sir. We can easily accommodate eighteen horses plus their riders," Captain Bart said.

Millie came out of the cabin, but stood in the background listening to the men talk. She fervently hoped that whatever Captain Dickinson's mission was, it would not implicate her family. Fourteen-year-old Tammy stood next to her. She was completely focused on Charles Dickinson, the Captain's son, who she thought must be the most handsome man in the Confederate Army. Five years older than Tammy, the young sergeant thought she was very pretty and wistfully regretted the age difference. Who knows, he thought. Perhaps after the war in another couple years or so… In any event, Tammy coyly flirted with him and he winked back – all unseen by the others, except Tucker who smiled and shook his head in mock disapproval.

In less than an hour, the cavalry horses, their riders, ammunition and weapons were loaded onto the barge. The horses were securely tethered to the deck. However, it was unlikely there would be a problem with them since they were accustomed to crossing the St. Johns and other Florida rivers on flatboats as the War Eagle carried out his many raids on Union positions. Accompanying the cavalry contingent to the pier, Tucker told Lieutenant McEaddy that he truly would like to go with them. The lieutenant explained that this particular mission required expert horsemen. However, he said, contrary to common understanding, not all men in a cavalry company needed to be expert riders. He said they were always looking for good men and that Tucker should talk to Corporal Piggot about his interest. Piggot and the five other men would be remaining at the Beckham homestead the remainder of the day.

The area around the pier was now crowded. Jessie, Millie, Tucker and Tammy were all down at the landing together with Corporal Piggot and the five cavalrymen who were remaining at the homestead. Jessie and Tucker cast off the lines that were then hauled aboard by Amos and Shane. Captain Bart gave an order to Henry and a loud hiss of steam was heard as the piston was forced through the cylinder and began revolving the paddlewheel. The six cavalrymen at the pier all snapped to attention and saluted, knowing that their comrades would soon be engaged in a dangerous firefight. Captain Dickinson acknowledged their salute on behalf of the men on the barge and returned it smartly. Millie waved and Tammy began to cry.

As the barge began moving up the river, Corporal Piggot posted a guard at the pier and then marched the rest of his squad back to the area where the remaining animals were tethered and grazing. Later, he approached Tucker and said, "Hey Tucker, someone said you know how to shoot a musket."

Tucker was amused. He more than knew how to handle a musket. However, in a reserved manner he simply said, "Yep. At least I know how to keep from shooting my own ass off."

Piggot laughed and replied, "Well, we'll be here for a few more hours. How about you and me seeing how well you can shoot?"

Tucker readily accepted the challenge and the two went to set up a makeshift target range. They set up a line of old coffee tins stuck on posts at a distance of 50, 100 and 200 yards from where they intended to shoot. Each man took a Springfield Model 1861 muzzle loaded musket, a supply of cartridges and prepared to load his weapon. One of the cavalrymen observing the contest held up a pocket watch so that he could time how rapidly the muskets were fired.

On the timer's command, both Piggot and Tucker loaded their weapons. They both followed the same procedure. First, they took a cartridge from a pouch and bit off one end. Next, they poured the powder down the musket barrel, followed by the 58-caliber ball that was at the end of the cartridge and then they rammed powder, ball and cartridge paper firmly down the barrel. Next, they half-cocked the hammer, took a firing cap out of the cap box in the musket's stock and placed it in the cone of the musket. At the ready command, they full cocked the hammer.

There would be a total of six rounds, two per target at the designated range beginning with the targets at 50 yards. At the command fire, both men fired and hit their targets. They reloaded as fast as they could and fired again, hitting the 50-yard target a second time. Continuing to reload and fire, it seemed that Tucker was gaining a few seconds on the corporal as both men fired and hit the 100-yard targets, Tucker clearly hitting his first. Another reload and although both men hit their targets, Tucker clearly had fired first and was reloading before the corporal. Then, while the corporal was still reloading, Tucker fired and hit his 200-yard target. The corporal fired, missed and began to reload. However, Tucker had already fired his second round hitting his target. Then, in a burst of speed, Tucker reloaded his musket and fired an instant before the corporal this time hitting Piggot's target blowing it off the pole.

"Hot damn!" Corporal Piggot shouted. "That was some shooting!"

The private who had been timing the contest said, "I can't believe it, Toby. He fired at the rate of five rounds per minute. Crack infantry doesn't do any better than that."

"Tucker, you and I need to have a little talk," Piggot said. What Tucker did not yet know was that Lieutenant McEaddy had instructed the corporal to test Tucker on his ability to handle and fire a Springfield. One of the needs that Company H had was for sharpshooters. Without realizing it, Tucker had just more than qualified for that role.

Later that afternoon, as the cavalry squad was preparing to leave the Beckham homestead, Tucker asked to speak with his mother and father privately. Jessie feared that he knew what was coming. The three sat down together at the dining table and Tucker, long-faced, told his parents that he was joining Captain Dickinson's cavalry company.

"Mama and Paw, this is something that I have to do. My conscience will not allow me to stay home here at Cracker Landing when other men my age are sacrificing their safety to protect the rest of us. You both raised me better than that," Tucker said.

Millie raised her apron to her eyes to wipe away the tears that were forming. Jessie's own eyes were moist as he burst with pride in his son. Both of them, however, were filled with apprehension for Tucker's safety.

"I know you both are worried that I might get hurt or worse. That is always possible. However, Corporal Piggot told me that he has been in several skirmishes and that there have been very few casualties on our side. The Yankees, however, have taken quite a beating!"

Instead of being as reassuring as Tucker intended, the mere mention of casualties made Millie's tears flow more freely. She wept softly while Jessie responded to Tucker.

"Son, you are eighteen years old – nineteen in just a couple of months. I could not stop you if I tried. However, this has to be your decision only. I just ask you to be certain this is what you want to do and if you do go with that man they call the War Eagle, keep your wits about you and shoot straight and true."

Tucker nodded and began to get up from the table when Tammy came in and asked what was happening.

"I'm going to join the army, little sister," Tucker said. Tammy burst into tears and hugged her big brother, begging him not to go. "I've got to," Tucker said. He got up, hugged his mother and father and then left to join Corporal Piggot who was waiting for him outside with the other cavalrymen.

Chapter Nineteen

Even though Jessie was tapping pinesap from the trees far beyond the crop field, he could easily hear the whistle of the steam barge approaching Cracker Landing. When the whistle sounded, Jessie pulled the tap from the tree he was working on and immediately went to the cabin to get Millie. However, she was already waiting for him at the head of the path leading down to the pier. Although Captain Bart stopped by Cracker Landing frequently, it had been a while since Jessie and Millie had seen Ellen and Millie's parents. Jessie knew that Millie was eager for news about them. By now, of course, all of the family knew that Tucker had joined the army.

"I wonder if Bart has heard anything about Tucker," Millie said.

"I sure hope so," Jessie replied. "However, I'd like to know how Ellen and your parents are as well." Millie nodded in agreement.

By the time the two got down to the river, Captain Bart and his crew had already secured the barge to the pier. A grim look was on his face when walked over the Jessie and Millie.

"Bell has done it again," he said in frustration, throwing his cap on the ground. He was referring to Colonel Louis Bell

149

who had been appointed the military commander of St. Augustine during the Union's occupation of the city.

"Done what Bart?" Jessie asked.

"Well, you know that the city has been under martial law imposed by that SOB for several months now. I believe you also know that ever since he declared martial law, he also has been requiring that anyone who wants to enter or leave the city be required to sign a loyalty pledge to the Federal government. He even has confiscated the homes and belongings of several women, whose husbands are currently fighting on the Confederate side, because they refused to sign that oath. He forced them to leave the city, too," He added.

"How terrible!" Millie exclaimed. "What did the poor women do?"

"I don't rightly know," Captain Bart said. "But, I can tell you that the women in the city are furious about it. That's not the worst of it. Up until now, none of the military bothered people like us transporting goods to and from the city. But now, they won't let us in the city, either, unless we sign that damn oath!" He was obviously furious.

"What are other people doing, Bart?" Jessie asked.

"A fair number of them are signing the oath. Some told me it's not worth the paper it's written on and they are only signing it so they can survive. But, others refuse to sign it."

"What happens to the ones who refuse to sign it?" Millie asked.

"Depends." Captain Bart answered. "If they live in the city, they can't get out and they also can't get ration coupons meaning they can't get the food they need. On the other hand, if the people who refuse to sign it already live out the city not much happens to them except they can't get in to do business or buy supplies."

"So, the biggest effect on all of us is that we can't get into the city to sell rosin and buy things like flour, coffee and other hard-to-get supplies, or, in your case, sell lumber," Jessie speculated. "How about Tucker? Have you heard anything about him?"

"Not directly. But I did find out that Captain Dickinson and his men whopped the Yankees real bad when they raided them at the old Fort Diego site."

"That's why they were here, then," Jessie surmised.

"Yep. When they got to the mill they headed on toward the fort where they Yankee patrol was camped out. The Yankees must have been lollygagging because they were caught by surprise. Two of them were killed, several wounded and a total of nine were captured. A handful reportedly got away."

"How about the War Eagle's casualties?" Jessie inquired. Millie shuddered at the mention of casualties.

Captain Bart laughed. "One of Dickinson's cavalry men got a busted arm from a minni ball and another sprained his ankle when his horse was shot out from under him. That's it!"

"But, no word about Tucker since that day?" Millie said.

"No, nothing," Captain Bart reiterated. "But, don't you worry, Millie. He is in good company and that fellow Dickinson is an able leader. Tucker will be just fine."

Millie turned to Jessie and said, "We need to go up to the mill to see all of them soon. I really miss them."

Jessie nodded and then said to his brother-in-law, "Bart, how do you folks at the mill feel about signing that oath?"

"We have no intention of doing it," Captain Bart said. "I'll tell you this, we are the closest sawmill to St. Augustine. It won't be long before they are begging us to sell them lumber – with or without an oath. How about you, Jessie?"

151

"How could we sign it? Our son is a soldier in the Confederate Army! We have our crops, our animals, the swamp and forest. We'll manage."

Tammy had been playing with Little Fox and his little sister, Little Flower. She walked over to see what the adults were talking about.

"Hello Uncle Bart," she said. "Have you heard anything about Tucker?"

"No I haven't, darl'n. Your maw and paw just asked me the same question."

"How about Sergeant Dickinson? Have you heard anything about him?"

"No, I haven't heard anything about him, either." Captain Bart asked. "Why do you ask?"

"Oh, I was just wondering," Tammy replied. "

Captain Bart looked at Jessie quizzically. "I'll tell you about that later," Jessie said. "Do you have time for a quick snort of Lightning?"

"I'll make time for that!" Captain Bart chuckled. He waved to Amos and Shane and they followed him, Jessie and Millie up to the cabin.

***

A grim Captain J. J. Dickinson listened to the report of Lola Sanchez, a confederate spy who lived with her two sisters in Palatka, a port city on the St. Johns River. Lola became a Confederate spy when the Union mistakenly accused her father of spying for the Confederacy and imprisoned him in Fort Marion. Union soldiers now occupied the Sanchez residence to keep an eye on the family. However, one night, after preparing dinner for Union officers, Lola overheard their plan to send the Union gunboat USS Columbine the next morning to capture

152

Captain Dickinson and the men of his Company H. With the help of her sisters, Lola escaped from the house and rode to Dickinson's camp to warn him of the impending danger.

"How did you come about this information, Lola?" Captain Dickinson asked.

"Ever since the Yankees occupied our house, we have had to prepare dinner for them," Lola explained. "Tonight there were two Yankee officers at the house and while serving them dinner I heard about their plan to capture you and your men tomorrow morning."

"You say they think we are in Welaka," Dickinson said.

"That's right, sir. They plan on taking the gunboat with over one hundred soldiers aboard to Welaka, debark the soldiers and surround you and your troops."

"Did they say who the commanding officer of the Yankees is?"

"They did. It is Colonel William Nobel of the 17th Connecticut Infantry."

"Lola, you did a mighty fine job and we are very grateful to you and your sisters. Do you think you can get back to your house safely?"

"I believe so, Captain. I just hope you and your men will be safe."

"With the information you have given us, I believe we will be just fine. Now you had better be getting back to Palatka."

As soon as Lola left, Dickinson ordered Lieutenant McCardell to rouse the men and tell them to prepare to mount up immediately. He intended to turn tables on Colonel Noble and his soldiers.

153

Within an hour, thirty of the War Eagle's cavalry men, including Tucker Beckham who was now one of Dickinson's sharpshooters, left their camp and headed to a location on the west side of the St. Johns River called Horse Landing, located on the opposite shore five miles upriver from Welaka. Towed behind the cavalry unit were two twelve-pounder brass rifled cannons borrowed from the artillery company called Milton's Light Artillery.

Dickinson selected Horse Landing to ambush the Union gunship because at that spot ships had to come within sixty yards of the west bank of the river. Further, there were dense woods and shrubs on the riverbank that made excellent cover for the troops. Arriving before dawn, Dickinson's men, including the cannons, were in position well before the gunship passed by.

"How you doing, Private Tucker?" Corporal Piggot asked.

"Just fine, Toby. "I'm so comfortable snuggled in these bushes that I just might take a nap," Tucker joked.

"Oh yeah," Piggot said. "That would be a good way to wind up with a Yankee minni ball in your britches! Want a chew?" he asked offering Tucker a twist of tobacco.

"Actually, I hate the stuff," Tucker responded. "Wouldn't mind a little of my paw's Cracker Landing Lightning, though," he said.

Sergeant Dickinson passed down the line of men positioned in the woods making sure that all were ready and alert.

"On the ready, men," he said. Our scout just rode in and said the gunboat is about a mile and a half up river. It should pass by here in another ten minutes."

Then, the young Dickinson came over to Tucker and said, "Tucker, we need to disable the gunboat as quickly as possible. I want you to concentrate on the wheelhouse. If you can see anything moving inside it or if anyone enters or leaves – take them out. If you can't see anyone then use your best judgement for alternate targets."

"Understood, sergeant," Tucker said as he made sure his Springfield was loaded and primed. It would only take the gunboat a short time to pass Horse Landing. Tucker would have to make full use of his skill in reloading and shooting the musket.

The USS Columbine was a 117 foot converted side paddle tugboat built in 1850. It had a top speed of twelve miles per hour and normally carried a compliment of twenty-five officers and enlisted men. It was armed with two, twenty-pound parrot rifled cannons. Because of its mission this day, the gunboat also carried a compliment of 148 soldiers from Colonel Noble's regiment. As the Columbine approached the bend at Horse Landing, it reduce speed to only five miles per hour so that it could safely navigate the shallow channel curved around the bend.

"It's coming!" Sergeant Dickinson shouted. His father calmly watched the approaching gunboat as it approached closer and closer to the shore where they were positioned. When it was at its closest point, he gave the order to begin the attack.

Shots rang out from the shore as startled Union soldiers aboard the ship did the best they could to take cover. The problem was that the gunboat was now clearly visible against the rising sun in the east while Dickinson's cavalry were well hidden among the trees and scrub brush. Tucker's sights were focused on the wheelhouse, but he could not see anyone inside and no one tried to leave or enter it.

The boom of the Milton artillery sounded. One of the cannon shots struck the stern of the vessel while another must have hit a boiler steam line because the paddle wheel slowly ground to a stop. Just then, Tucker saw two sailors rush to the parrot guns and swivel them toward shore. He took careful aim at one of them, pulled the trigger and saw the sailor spin around and fall to the deck. Before he could reload, a shell from the second parrot gun exploded no more than fifty feet from his position, splintering a tall pine tree and sending the top half crashing to the ground.

By now, gunfire from the gunboat was beginning to pepper the shore with small arms fire. However, Dickinson's men were well dug in and the gunfire had little effect on them. Tucker took aim at the sailor manning the second parrot gun, fired and the man fell back onto the deck.

After forty-five minutes, it was all over. The Columbine could not be steered, it had no propulsion and ran aground. Acting ensign Frank Sandborn went ashore and surrendered the ship to Captain Dickinson. Colonel Noble was wounded in the shoulder. Half of the crew of the Columbine were wounded and one sailor was killed. Dickinson's men suffered no casualties.

Chapter Twenty

SATURDAY AFTERNOON DINNER at the Sutter's house was a special family occasion. It had been a month since Millie and Jessie had seen Millie's parents and Jessie's sister Ellen. Tammy, in particular, was thrilled to see her grandparents and her Aunt Ellen. But, the best news was they learned Tucker was alright. In fact, when Captain Bart made a recent trip downriver to deliver lumber supplies, he learned that Tucker was some sort of local hero. According to what he had been told, Tucker's sharpshooting skills saved the lives of many of the men in his company by taking the Columbine's two parrot cannons out of action. He also learned that the War Eagle's men burned and sank the Columbine to prevent it being used again by the Yankees. While that was good news for the residents of the area who were sympathetic toward the Confederate cause, it was bad news for the occupying Union forces and for Yankee sympathizers.

Cracker Landing Lightning was flowing freely at the Sutter dinner table and Tom Sutter raised a half-filled glass of it in a toast. "Here's to Tucker and the brave men of Company H," he said. Everyone raised their glass and cheered. "Here's to Captain J. J. Dickinson, the War Eagle," Jessie said as he raised his glass. Everyone joined in that toast as well. Captain Bart was the last one to make a toast. "And, here is to the

157

Confederate States of America," he said. Everyone stood up, raised their glasses and began to sing the popular southern song "Dixie." There was no question where their sympathies were.

After more merriment, the family sat down to a dinner more sparse than ones they had previously enjoyed. Although the Beckham homestead was still producing enough food for them to get by, the family was experiencing many of the same problems that other homesteaders faced. Some homesteads still had chickens, but much of the domestic livestock had been killed to provide food for the military. Woodlands more accessible to foraging troops on both sides had been stripped of much of their wildlife. The Beckhams, on the other hand, had several advantages over many other families in the region. Their homestead abutted abundant coastal waters including the river, marsh and estuaries that continued to provide oysters, clams and other mollusks and fish. Wild hogs still roamed the swamps and woodlands, as did wild turkey and deer, albeit in lesser quantities than before the war. Although flour and sugar were in short supply, corn (and thus cornmeal), sweet potatoes, squash and beans were among the foodstuff that they could still cultivate, grow and process. "City folk," such as the residents of St. Augustine, did not have such advantages.

After an early dinner, it was time to return to Cracker Landing. Goodbyes were said and then Jessie, Millie and Tammy boarded Captain Bart's steam barge. Ellen came aboard, also, for the ride. Soon they were on their way toward the landing, several miles downstream.

"Bart, I feel guilty that you are using the sawmill barge just to take us back to the landing," Jessie lamented.

"No, no. It is not the sawmill's barge," Captain Bart replied. "I work for the sawmill, but I own the barge. That was the deal I made when I first came down here from Savannah. They had just started building the barge when I arrived. I told

Mr. Finnegan – now General Finnegan, of course – that I wanted to buy it. He laughed and said he doubted I could afford $2,000. He stopped laughing when I put up $1,000 and said he could take the rest out of my pay."

Millie was puzzled. "Why did you want to buy a barge, Bart?"

"Well, I figured that someday I would take it back up to Savannah and run it from there to cotton and indigo plantations upriver and then downriver to Hilton Head. Alternatively, I could ply the St. Johns River between plantations."

Amos shouted out that Cracker Landing was in sight. He said it looked like the two Seminoles were standing on the pier waiting for them.

"That's strange," Jessie said. "I can't imagine why they would be waiting for us there – unless something is wrong!"

Approaching the pier, they could hear Little Fox wailing in pain. Anna was trying to console him but she also had Little Flower to contend with. Joseph did the best he could to help his wife, but Little Fox wanted his mother.

While the men were still securing the barge to the pier, Ellen, Millie and Tammy ran to see what was wrong with Little Fox. In horror, they could see that his left leg was bent back in an unnatural position.

"I was feeding the chickens and the children were playing on your porch," Anna explained. "I heard a lot of laughter and when I looked up I saw that Little Fox had climbed up on your roof. Before I could even warn him, he slipped, fell off and landed on his left leg. See how it is bent," she wailed. "It must be broken!"

In all of the time they had been at Cracker Landing, none of the Beckham's had ever experienced a fracture or broken bone. However, Captain Bart had seen his share of that type of injury because of the hazardous nature of work done at the sawmill and on ships he had sailed. He gingerly moved his hand at the site of Little Fox's injury and looked up at the worried crowd around him.

"I think we need to get him to a doctor as soon as possible. It's pretty badly injured. Look how swollen it is. It needs to be set and then put into a splint. At his age, Little Fox is growing real fast. If we set the leg the wrong way, he might never walk properly.

There was no further discussion. Everyone sprang into action. Captain Bart shouted orders to Henry to squeeze as much steam as he could out of the boiler. Amos and Shane began to haul in the lines even as everyone else jumped aboard the barge. In less than five minutes, the barge was headed full speed downriver toward St. Augustine where the nearest doctor was located. Meanwhile, Little Fox alternated between sharp screams of pain and more muted moaning. The men paced around the deck while the women did their best to console Anna and Little Fox. Tammy took charge of Little Flower. Joseph stopped pacing, stood with his arms uplifted and began praying.

Three hours later, after a harrowing trip in darkness downriver, the steam barge entered St. Augustine harbor. It was due only to the piloting skill of Captain Bart and the navigating assistance of his crew that the barge did not run into the shallows or a sandbar or hit a floating log in the mad dash to the city. In truth, a clear sky and a half moon helped considerably.

After the barge was secured to the city pier, Captain Bart sent Amos to the harbormaster's office to learn where the nearest doctor could be found. Abner Cranston, the harbormaster was fast asleep when Amos pounded on the door of the building that was both Cranston's residence and office. Unhappy to be waken in the middle of the night, Cranston suggested they go to the residence of Dr. Nathaniel Benedict on Marine Street, not far from the old St. Francis Barracks where Union soldiers were now housed. "Don't expect that he is going to be happy about being waken up at this time of the night," Cranston shouted as Amos ran back to the pier."

Within minutes, the entire Beckham family plus Joseph, Anna, Little Fox and Little Flower were on their way to Dr. Benedict's house. Captain Bart and his crew remained with the barge.

Dr. Benedict's residence was a large two-storied coquina house with a wide, pillared porch set back from the street between two large live oak trees. It was also his medical office. The house was in total darkness when Jessie and entourage arrived. Jessie knocked on the door of the doctor's residence loudly. There was no response. He knocked again – more loudly. And, then again. Finally, a light was seen within the house as someone lit a lamp. A few moments later, an elderly Negro woman, opened the door and stared at the sight before her. There was Jessie, Millie, Ellen, Tammy and, behind them, Joseph, Anna and the two children, the latter who were all dressed in traditional Seminole clothing. Little Fox, now completely exhausted and spent, was moaning and whimpering. It must have been a shocking sight because the woman who had opened the door put her hand to her mouth and screamed.

An elderly man with a long white beard came up behind her to see what the problem was. He was dressed in a nightshirt and a pair of spectacles sat low on the bridge of his nose.

"What the world is going on?" he demanded, looking almost as shocked as his housekeeper.

Jessie began to describe what happened, but could not seem to get the story straight. Ellen took over and gave the doctor a brief explanation of how Little Fox got hurt.

"Bring him in to this room," the doctor said pointing to a room filled with an indescribable array of medical equipment that terrified Joseph and Anna. "The parents can come in, however, the rest of you stay outside on the porch! I don't have room for a whole damn Cracker family," he said gruffly.

Once inside his examining room, Dr. Benedict again asked Anna and Joseph what happened to the boy. After Anna explained how the accident happened, the doctor examined Little Fox's leg. The boy screamed whenever the doctor touched the most swollen areas.

"It is not likely that he broke his leg entirely," the doctor said. "He probably has what is called a 'greenstick' fracture. In children his age, the leg usually bends and then slightly fractures on the stress side. However, I have to set it and then he will have to wear a splint."

Anna nodded her head while Joseph simply looked he son helplessly. "Will that hurt?" Anna asked.

"Setting the leg, yes. But not the splint," Dr. Benedict said. "I must use an anesthetic before I can set the leg. Bring him into my office and put him on the table over there," he said pointing to a padded table.

Neither Anna nor Joseph had any idea what an anesthetic was. "I will use something called chloroform to put him to sleep while I set the leg," the doctor explained. "He will be just fine," he added reassuringly.

A half-hour later, Anna walked out onto the porch of the doctor's house carrying Little Fox who was very groggy. His left leg was held firm by a pre-carved wood splint Dr. Benedict had selected from several he kept in reserve just for this type of incident. A heavy wrap of bandage surrounded the splint and the leg.

"He will have to wear the splint for at least three weeks," Dr. Benedict said "Bring him back then so that I can see if the fracture has healed properly. There should be no problem. Children heal twice as fast as adults."

The question of payment was on everyone's mind – except the doctor's. Awkwardly, Jessie pulled a few confederate dollars out of his pocket and offered them to the doctor.

"What the hell is that?" Dr. Benedict said, knowing full well that he was looking at confederate money.

"Uh, we want to pay you for what you did, but I don't know how much?" Jessie said with embarrassment.

"It's not how much, son," the elderly man said. "Don't you know that nobody in this town accepts confederate money anymore? Where have you been this past year?"

Jessie was perplexed. The fact was he had not been in the city for several months – ever since Tucker left to join Captain Dickinson's cavalry company. Moreover, ever since the war began, he bartered the turpentine Captain Bart took to the city on his behalf for supplies he and Millie needed. There was no actual exchange of money.

Dr. Benedict could see that Jessie was completely flustered. "Tell me, why do you want to pay for the boy's treatment? Who are these Indians to you, anyway?"

Jessie did not know what to say. "They were your slaves, weren't they?" Dr. Benedict surmised.

Jessie nodded. "But, only because there was no other way they could stay and work on my farm. They told me that if I did not register them as slaves, they would be relocated to Oklahoma against their will," he explained.

Dr. Benedict dropped his gruffness and said, "I understand. Well, they are not slaves now. Ever since the Yankees occupied this city, things have changed. You Crackers haven't been affected by the war as much as those of us who live

163

in the city. For example, you will never be able to use confederate script in this part of the state again. Whatever you do for a living, you better make sure you get paid in Yankee script or, better yet, in gold."

Doctor Benedict turned to go back into his house. "By the way, I do not charge for treating children as young as the boy," he said. Then he stopped and turned to Anna and Joseph. "One more thing," he said. "Do not let him climb back on that damn roof again!" He opened the front door, but paused just before he entered the house. Turning to them again, he added, "Or even a tree!"

As the first light of dawn began to break over the Ancient city, the exhausted Beckhams, Joseph, Anna and their children made their way back to the city pier. Captain Bart and his crew helped them board the sawmill barge where they collapsed in a tired heap. A few minutes later, Captain Bart gave the order to his crew to cast off lines and open the steam lines. It was time to head back upriver to Cracker Landing.

Chapter Twenty-One

ALL HE COULD SEE WAS a blur of light. However, the pain was still there. He remembered when he was a young boy and made the mistake of walking too close behind the mule he had been trying to hitch to the plow. The ornery critter kicked him and sent him flying half way across the barn. Luckily, he got kicked in the shoulder instead of his head. That's how the pain felt now. Maybe even worse. He unsuccessfully tried to raise his head and then slipped back into darkness.

"I think he's trying to wake up!" Ellie Westcott said to her cousin Lucy Dancy. Tenderly, she wiped the perspiration from the wounded cavalryman's forehead and then laid a damp compress on it to cool his fever.

Ellie and her mother Amanda, a widow, were forced to leave St. Augustine over a year ago. Colonel Bell, commanding officer of the occupying Union troops in the city, learned they had helped smuggle foodstuff out of the city to supply Confederate soldiers who had been harassing Union patrols. Bell confiscated their home on St. Francis Street and ordered them to leave the city with only those possessions they could take on a wagon. Ever since that tragedy, they had been living with Amanda's sister Elizabeth Dancy on the Dancy farm outside of Palatka, just east of the St. Johns River.

The area in which the Dancy home was situated was essentially under the control of Confederate Captain J. J. Dickinson, except for one homestead nearby that was frequented by Union officers. That was the homestead of Don Mauricio Sanchez who was confined to prison at Fort Marion when he was falsely accused of spying for the rebels. Unknown to those officers, however, Panchita (also called Lola), one of the three Sanchez sisters, was herself a spy for the War Eagle and kept him supplied with information she overheard from the officers' conversations. On one recent occasion, Lola's information enabled Dickinson to capture and burn the Union gunboat Columbine.

Tucker coughed and immediately winced at the pain that wracked the entire upper right side of his torso. He opened his eyes and tried to focus on the figures standing over him. There were two women, but he still could not make out their faces through the blur that prevented his eyes from clearly seeing them.

"Corporal Beckham, my name is Lucy Dancy and this is my cousin Ellie Westcott. We have to change your bandage and it is going to hurt. I am sorry."

A gentle hand wiped the perspiration from his forehead and then he felt more pain as one of the women – he could not tell which one – unwrapped and removed the old poultice from the fleshy part of his right shoulder. The two women struggled to lift him into a half-sitting position and then there was a searing pain as Ellie placed a damp cloth folded to form a poultice on the open wound. The women quickly wrapped a fresh bandage over the fresh poultice and around his torso to hold it in place.

Now beginning to focus his eyes better, Tucker sputtered, "What the devil did you put on my shoulder? It feels like a hot poker!"

"It is bromine. The doctor said it will help prevent an infection," Ellie explained. "I'm sorry it hurt so badly."

"Do you want to sit up or lay back down?" Lucy asked.

"Where am I?" Tucker asked, noting that he was in a small, windowless room half-sitting up on an army cot with a pillow propping his back." Then he remembered.

The War Eagle had been successful in maintaining Confederate control of the counties west of the St. Johns River. Then, on the morning of August 6, 1864, Dickinson and thirty of his Cavalry men, including Tucker Beckham and Dickinson's son Sergeant Charles Dickinson, encountered a force of 178 Union cavalry at Nine Mile Swamp west of Palatka. The fighting was fierce – at one point Dickinson's men were in hand-to-hand combat with the Yankees. Tucker recalled that he had dismounted from his horse and was trying to reload his musket. However, the fighting was too close quarters so he held the musket by the barrel and used it as a club, bashing a Union soldier in the head. That's when Tucker looked up and saw a Union lieutenant cock his revolver and aim it at him. The next instant, a tremendous force struck him in the right shoulder throwing him back and onto the ground. The last sight he remembered before passing out was a mist of blood enveloping the Union lieutenant's head as the officer slumped forward in his saddle.

Tucker repeated his question to the woman named Lucy, "Where am I and how did I get here?"

"You are on a cot in a spare room of my house, the Dancy home," Lucy said. "You were brought here laying across the saddle of a horse by my brother, James."

167

"Your brother? Wait. Is James Dancy your brother?"

"He is, indeed. I take it you know him."

"Of course, he and I are both in Captain Dickinson's Company."

"Why did James bring me here?" Tucker asked.

"Well, let's say that you are not the first wounded member of Captain Dickinson's Company H who spent a little time in this house," Ellie replied smiling. "The Dancy home is quite near Captain Dickinson's camp."

"You mean the one at Ralston on the bank of the river?" Tucker surmised. He had been stationed at that camp.

"Yes, that's the one," Ellie confirmed. "We are only about a mile away from the Sanchez residence where the Yankees have stationed a guard because they suspect the Sanchez girls are spies for our side."

"And here we Dancy ladies are, right under the Yankees' noses, taking care of one of the Captain's men," Lucy giggled.

"With a Yankee guard so close, aren't you afraid of being caught?" Tucker wondered.

"Not likely," Ellie said. She pointed to a large chest next to the cot and smiled. "There is a trap door under that chest. If the Yankees came by, down you would go under the house!"

"What's down there?"

"Nothing nice. But if anyone looked under the house from outside all they would see is part of the foundation."

"Who wrapped up my shoulder?" Tucker asked.

"A good rebel doctor, first," Lucy said. "He gave us a bottle of bromine to put on the wound and told us to change your bandage twice a day until it began to heal."

"You are very lucky," Ellie stated solemnly. "There was one other casualty of that skirmish ya'll had with the Yankees. Captain Dickinson lost his son Charles."

Tucker sat up like he was hit by a bolt of lightning. "Charles! Sergeant Charles is dead?" he said, not believing what he just heard.

"Sadly, yes," Lucy replied. "It was quite terrible, too. Apparently, it seemed that the Yankees had surrendered and several of them were taken as prisoners. But, no one noticed that some of them were hiding their weapons and suddenly they started shooting. Sergeant Dickinson was shot in the heart and died almost instantly. He fell in the arms of his friend Joe Larkin who had just dismounted from his own horse. The Captain is in deep grieving."

"There were only two of you shot in the skirmish – you and Sergeant Dickinson," Ellie added sadly. Then angrily she added, "But you best know that those damn Yankees got their proper up 'n comin's for what they did!"

Tucker immediately thought of Tammy. He knew she had a crush on Charles. How was he going to tell her that Charles was dead, he wondered. What a tragedy. Besides, Charles had been a good friend and had taught him a lot about soldiering. He felt a strong urge to rejoin his Company and revenge Charles's death. Oh, dear God, he thought. The Captain must be truly stricken by his death. He tried to get out of bed but then discovered that he could not move his right arm without terrible pain in the shoulder.

"Tucker! What are you trying to do?" Ellie practically shouted. "The doctor said that you have to keep that arm still until the wound completely heals. You took a minni ball in your shoulder and the doctor had to pluck it out. He said it could easily become infected and then he'd have to amputate it."

The thought of losing his arm was enough to persuade Tucker to follow his nurses' instructions. He nodded in understanding and then noticed that Ellie, who had just scolded him severely was now smiling at him. What beautiful brown eyes she has, he thought. And, her hair. It was a light chestnut color, parted in the middle and tied in a bun behind her head. It framed her face perfectly.

"What are you looking at?" She asked.

"Oh, sorry. I was just thinking."

"About what?"

"Uh, nothing, I mean nothing important. Listen, ladies, I truly appreciate you both taking care of me, but when can I get back to my Company?"

"The doctor said he'd be back in a week or so," Lucy said. "So, until then you will be our guest. You will just have to put up with Ellie, me and both our mothers. Now, Ellie and I have to go and tend to the farm. When the Union soldiers first raided this side of the river, the Negros we had working the farm ran off and joined the Union Army. Now, we have to make do with the labor of just us four women."

Ellie came over to Tucker, bent over and gave him a kiss on the forehead. Then, she and Lucy left the room leaving Tucker to wonder what that was all about – not that he minded it one bit.

Chapter Twenty-Two

DOCTOR IRA HAWTHORNE GENTLY removed the gauze bandage covering Tucker's shoulder wound. He examined the wound carefully and then glanced over at Lt. M. J. McEaddy who had accompanied him to the Dancy home. Lt. McEaddy looked at the wound and then back at Dr. Hawthorne, shaking his head. Fortunately, Tucker did not see their look of concern. He was smiling at Ellie, who was holding his right hand, comforting him.

Dr. Hawthorne cleared his throat, "Corporal, I am afraid that your wound is becoming infected. I hoped the bromide would stop any infection. However, minni ball wounds are seldom clean. Rather than pass through the flesh, assuming the ball does not strike bone, they tend to lodge in the body until removed with a probe. That increases the chance for infection. In your case, I was able to remove the minni ball fragment. However, I could not remove any particles of dirt or cloth that might have caused the infection."

"I do not mind the bromide, doctor. You can put as much of it on my shoulder as you need to," Tucker said.

"Tucker, the problem is that the bromide does not seem to be working. If the infection worsens, gangrene might set in," the doctor explained.

"That's bad, isn't it?" Tucker asked, trying to hide his concern."

"Very bad, I'm afraid. Gangrene can be fatal. I can amputate an arm or leg if gangrene sets in but I cannot amputate a shoulder," Dr. Hawthorne said.

"You mean that I might die," Tucker stated as calmly as possible.

"Yes, son. You might die," the doctor answered.

"Corporal, you have done your duty bravely and to the fullest," Lt. McEaddy said. "All of us are very proud of you."

Ellie understood the gravity of the situation and began weeping silently. Tucker looked at her and squeezed her hand more tightly. "I'll be OK, Ellie. You are a good nurse."

Ellie nodded and promised that she would take good care of him; but she could not hide the worry on her face. In addition, it was obvious to anyone that something more than a nurse – patient relationship was beginning to develop between the two of them.

"Tucker, do you like onions and garlic?" Dr. Hawthorne asked.

"Yes sir. My maw always puts them both in the soups and stews she makes."

"Good. We are going to continue to apply bromide to your wound. I know it hurts like hell, but you have been through a lot worse."

"Yes sir," Tucker replied. "I sure can deal with that OK. But, I don't understand why you asked if I like onions and garlic."

"Well, native people in different countries have used both of them for many years to help stop infections. So, in addition to the bromide, here is what we are going to do."

Dr. Hawthorne then turned to Ellie and her cousin Lucy who had just entered the room. He told them that they were to fetch an ample supply of both onions and garlic. He said that Tucker was to eat at least two raw onions a day as well as several raw garlic cloves. In addition, he told them that they were to cut the garlic cloves into thin slices and place the slices on the wound every time they changed the bandage.

"He's not going to smell pretty," Dr. Hawthorne said. "However, gangrene smells worse and we're going to try to stop that from happening."

Lt. McFaddy ordered Tucker to remain at the Dancy home. He said he and Dr. Hawthorne would return in another two weeks. Tucker pleaded to be allowed to return to Company H. However, he stopped protesting when the lieutenant reminded him that he had just been given an order.

***

They walked hand-in-hand along the rutted farm road that ran past the Dancy home between Palatka and Old Sulfur Spring to the north. Even though it was just early spring, the day was hot and humid with no sign of relief – except the inevitable brief afternoon thunderstorm. Tucker's right arm was strapped to his side to prevent any movement that might cause his shoulder wound to reopen. Before Dr. Hawthorne left the Dancy house, he made sure that both Lucy and Ellie knew how to immobilize Tucker's arm by wrapping long strips of gauze tightly around his upper chest and, of course, his arm. Tucker did have partial use of his right arm, however. He could raise and lower it below the elbow. However, even that caused some distress in his shoulder, as did his attempts to rapidly clench and release his right hand. Dr. Hawthorne had warned him that recovery would be long and sometimes painful. But, there was no real alternative.

Earlier that morning, Ellie told Tucker that she was going to take him to a special place. "What place? Where?" Tucker asked. "Oh, some place you will like," she replied. "It's just a little bit up the road." A "little bit" turned out to be two miles. However, there was so much to talk about and to share between them that neither was mindful of distance or time. Ellie was dressed in a light, loose fitting yellow cotton dress. She wore a bonnet of the same color that shaded her from the intense rays of the sun. Her right hand was nestled in Tucker's left hand. She carried a cloth covered wicker basket in the crook of her left arm. Tucker thought she looked incredibly beautiful. He felt almost out of place walking next to her. In contrast to Ellie's elegance, Tucker had an unshaven appearance and a well-worn cavalry jacket was draped over his shoulders. Shading him from the sun was a soiled, gray, broad brimmed felt hat seated low on his head.

For nearly an hour, they had been following an old farm road that paralleled the St. Johns River. Tucker noticed that the elevation of the road seemed to be rising as they proceeded northward. Then they came upon a path that led from the road toward the river. Ellie tugged Tucker's hand gently and led him along the path for a few yards until they stood on a bluff overlooking a horseshoe bend in the river. It looked all too familiar to Tucker. Yes, Ellie said, seeing the glint of recognition in Tucker's eyes. If you followed the bluff to the western most bend of the river, you would be at the site of the battle where the Union gunboat Columbine had been sunk by Captain Dickinson's cavalry, including a sharpshooter named Tucker Beckham. Tucker closed his eyes for a moment and visualized exactly where he, the Captain's son Charles and Toby Piggot were hiding in the brush as they carefully took aim at the Union crew manning the parrot guns firing at them and their comrades.

174

"Is this what you wanted me to see?" Tucker asked. "This is the special place you told me about?"

"No, but it is near here. Come on, follow me," she said laughingly as she tugged his hand. She led him down from the bluff to a place where a creek feeding the river ended in a natural pool. "This is the place," she said. "It is a spring that feeds the creek that flows into the river."

Tucker noticed the odor of sulfur in the air. "It's a sulfur spring," he observed.

"Uh huh," she said in agreement. "If we followed the farm road another five miles we would reach a small town called Old Sulfur Spring. People go there to bathe in the spring because they claim the water has a special healing power. Some say that the sulfur in the water helps relieve aching muscles. Others say that it helps heal infections. This is a much smaller spring," she added. "Most people do not even know it is here,"

They found a place where the grass along the edge of the spring was matted down. Ellie put down the wicker basket and removed the cloth cover, which she spread on the grass like a tablecloth. Tucker noted that the basket contained bread, cold meat, fruit and a flask. Under the food, however, was a roll of gauze and, of course, a raw onion and garlic cloves.

"Your choice," Ellie said, as they sat down together. "Would you like to eat first and then take a dip in the spring or vice versa?"

"Take a dip in the spring!" Tucker exclaimed. "You want me to get in the water?"

"Well, I most certainly do. I'm supposed to be your nurse. One of them, anyway," she said. "Don't worry. First, I'll remove your bandage and save as much of the gauze as I can. After you bathe I'll wrap you up again – and yes, in addition to the onion and garlic, I brought a small bottle of bromide with me to put on your wound."

"Ellie, why are you doing this?" Tucker asked.

Ellie looked into his eyes and softly said, "Because I want so much for you to get better."

They looked at each other for another long minute and then, impulsively, Tucker pulled her close to him with his left arm and gently kissed her. They held the kiss, savoring it, and then kissed passionately until Tucker winced in pain. Ellie pulled back from him, "Oh Tucker. You didn't hurt your wound, did you?" she asked worriedly.

"It's OK," he said. "I just pulled it a little. I'll be fine." And, then to prove he was alright, he pulled her close to him again and they kissed once more – somewhat less forcefully this time."

Ellie pushed Tucker back and again asked whether he wanted to eat lunch or bathe in the sulfur spring first. Tucker chose the spring. So, Ellie told Tucker to remove his jacket and shirt. She took a pair of scissors from the basket and carefully cut the gauze holding the bandage covering his wound. She saved as much of the gauze as possible to rewrap the wound later. Then she removed the bandage and examined the wound. The garlic slices had helped seal the wound so that it was no longer open. Perhaps it was wishful thinking, however it seemed to her that some healing was taking place.

"Ellie, I can't get in the spring with my clothes on," Tucker pointed out.

"Of course not, silly. Go ahead, take them off. I won't peek!" She laughed at his awkwardness.

Tucker shed his clothes and slipped into the spring. It was shallow at that point – only three or four feet deep. The water felt refreshingly cool and soothing. He submerged his right shoulder, keeping his right arm as rigid as possible. He was not sure whether the sulfur water was doing any good, but this was the first time he had been able to immerse his whole body in water in weeks. He could almost feel the grime and sweat melt away.

"How long am I supposed to stay here?" he asked Ellie.

"You can get out anytime you want, now. It's time for lunch, anyway."

"Promise you won't peek!"

"Sorry, I can't hear you," Ellie replied coyly.

A few minutes passed and then Ellie asked what was taking Tucker so long.

"It's hard getting my trousers on using only my left arm. And, my right shoulder hurts a bit," he answered.

Concerned that Tucker might have opened the wound, Ellie spun around.

Tucker, bare chested but otherwise clothed, stood before her laughing. "Ah ha, you did peek," he said.

"You are a terrible man!" Ellie said with exasperation. "That was not fair."

Tucker laughed and walked over to her, still dripping wet despite now wearing most of his clothes. He drew her to him with his left arm and noted that she did not resist in the least. Their kiss was sweet and tender – better than just passionate. I love this woman, he thought. I want her to be with me forever. He could tell by the look in her eyes that she loved him, too. I can't let her down, he thought. Then, in his mind, he prayed, as his mother Millie taught him, that the God who has the power to heal all wounds would heal his wound, also.

177

The hot summer sun quickly dried Tucker's clothes. Ellie applied bromide from the bottle Dr. Hawthorn gave her to his shoulder wound and packed it with thin slices of raw garlic. Then she applied a fresh bandage to cover the wound and used as much of the old gauze as practicable, together with gauze from the roll she brought with her, to wrap his shoulder once more in a rigid position.

"It's past time for lunch," Ellie said. She took two cloth napkins from the basket and filled each with slices of cold pork, boiled eggs, nuts, fruit and a slice of homemade bread. The flask she brought was filled with fresh water, since the strong taste of sulfur water from the spring made it essentially undrinkable. When they finished their lunch, Ellie said, "Tucker, I have a surprise for you."

Anticipating some other delicacy, Tucker asked what it might be. Ellie smiled at him, reached into the wicker basket and pulled out a peeled raw onion.

"Oh no!" Tucker exclaimed.

"Oh yes!" Ellie retorted. "Don't forget that Dr. Hawthorne ordered you to eat at least two raw onions each day. So, get to it, corporal!"

Reluctantly, Tucker took the onion from Ellie, closed his eyes, took a big bite of the vegetable and pretended to savor it as though it was the most delicious thing he had ever tasted. They looked at each other and broke out in laughter.

"At least your bath in the spring got rid of some of the garlic smell she said.

"Yeah, but now I smell of sulfur," he replied. Then, they both began laughing again.

***

178

As promised, Lt. McEaddy accompanied Dr. Hawthorne on his return visit to the Dancy home. He watched as Dr. Hawthorne once again removed Tucker's bandage and examined his wound. Ellie and Lucy were also in the room and together with Lt. McEaddy watched expectantly. This time there was a smile on the doctor's face.

"Corporal, I think the worst is behind us. These ladies must be taking good care of you. Other than smelling like a wagonload of garlic and onions –with a little sulfur thrown in for good measure – I believe you are going to be just fine."

There was a hoot and holler from Tucker and cries of joy from Ellie and Lucy who were hugging each other. Lt. McEaddy smiled.

"Wonderful!" Tucker exclaimed. "How soon can I return to my Company, Doctor?"

"That is another matter, Tucker," the doctor said in a serious tone. "Stand up and raise your right arm slowly as straight out as you can."

Tucker was sitting in a chair at the kitchen table. He rose from the table and tried to put his arm out straight. A grimace appeared on his face. Even that movement was obviously painful. He barely raised his arm upward another three or four inches when sweat broke out on his forehead and he sat down heavily in the chair, his arm collapsing. He looked up with eyes pleading for the doctor to tell him that it was not true – that he had not lost the use of his right arm.

As gently as he could, Dr. Hawthorne said, "Tucker, eventually you should regain the use of your right arm. But, it will take a while – perhaps a long while. So, you cannot return to Captain Dickinson's Company H or any other military unit. You cannot hold a musket, Tucker. And, it will likely be months before you can even work a plow.

179

Tucker looked at the lieutenant. "Sir, there is a lot around the camp that I can do, even with a bad arm. And, I promise, I will work on shooting with my left arm. You know I am a good shot."

"Corporal, even though our forces have beaten the Union Army at every major battle here in Florida, the war is not going well for the Confederacy. Captain Dickinson and our cavalry company are urgently needed in the north central part of the state to help prevent the Union from capturing the capital at Tallahassee," he explained. Then he took a deep breath and said, "It is time for you to go home, Corporal. You have earned the respect and admiration of all of your comrades. You are among the bravest of the brave."

The lieutenant's words pierced Tucker's heart like a sword. He knew that his time as a soldier was over. He struggled to stand one more time. Then, bending his right arm at the elbow and using his left hand to raise it, he did his best to salute the lieutenant and with tears in his eyes said, "Yes, sir. God bless you, Captain Dickinson and all of the men in Company H."

Lieutenant McEaddy saluted back and then sharply wheeled out of the room, followed by Dr. Hawthorne. However, all of this was more than Ellie could bear. She broke down in sobs and ran to Tucker's side throwing her arms around his neck. "Oh, Tucker. I love you so much," she said.

Lucy was in tears, herself. She stood in a corner of the room crying, her hands covering her face.

Tucker braced himself the best he could. He let his tired and pain-filled right arm fall limp at his side. But, with his good, left arm, pulled Ellie even closer to him.

"Ellie, I love you, too. It may be time for me to go back to Cracker Landing. But, I cannot imagine living without you. If you will have me, I want you to be at my side – forever. Marry me, Ellie. Marry me now before I have to go home."

Ellie threw her arms around Tucker's neck, kissing him and telling him that she was his and would always be. Lucy's tears turned to squeals of joy. She cupped her face with her hands and then when Ellie turned toward her, she warmly embraced her cousin. Tucker wiped his brow and eyes with the sleeve of his left arm. He walked to a window overlooking the front porch of the Dancy home. With Ellie back at his side, Tucker hung his head as he watched Lieutenant McEaddy and Dr. Hawthorne ride away from the Dancy home on their way back to The War Eagle's cavalry company and Tucker's former comrades.

Chapter Twenty-Three

IT WAS WELL PAST MIDNIGHT when Sarah Sutter's sleep was broken by a noise outside their house near the sawmill. Her husband Tom was still fast asleep, exhausted from another tiring day at the mill. She heard it again, the sound of a horse whinnying and then the barking of their hound Sadie.

"Tom! Wake up," she said, nudging her husband urgently. "Somebody's outside!"

Tom Sutter grunted for a moment then slid out of bed and quickly donned his overalls. He grabbed his Spencer lever-action repeating rifle from its rack on the bedroom wall, loaded a round into the chamber and flipped off the safety. Making sure that he could not be seen against a background of light, he carefully peered out of a corner of the front room window into the darkness outside.

"It's probably just a bear that spooked Sadie and one of the horses," he said. "I'll check outside."

"Tom, please be careful," Sarah said, mindful of the increasing number of incidents of Confederate deserters who had formed marauding bands in the area. She draped a nightgown over her shoulders and followed Tom into the front room of the house. The noise of a horse whinnying again – much closer, this time – broke their concentration. Sadie began barking louder and more forcefully.

183

Tom cracked the door open slowly. He walked out onto the broad wrap-around-porch of their double pen house, rifle at the ready. After a few moments, Sarah lit a lantern and came out on the porch next to him. Then, two horses with riders approached the house, breaking through the darkness.

"Hello grandpaw and Nana. It's me, Tucker. I'm sorry to bother you so late."

"Tucker!" Sarah exclaimed as she ran down the porch steps. She was echoed a moment later by Tom who flipped on the safety of his rifle, propped it against the porch railing and joined Sarah. He held the reins to Tucker's horse while he dismounted, noticing that Tucker favored his right arm that seemed to be stiff. Then it dawned on both of them that Tucker had brought along a guest. Sarah held up the lantern and they were both surprised to see it was a woman about the same age as Tucker.

Tucker hitched the reins of his horse to the post in front of the house while Tom took the reins of the other horse. Then Tucker turned to both of them, smiled broadly and said, "Nana and grandpaw, I want you to meet the newest member of our family – my wife Ellie!"

Tucker chuckled at the look on the faces of his grandparents, who were already in shock at his unexpected visit. They had not seen him in over a year since he joined Captain Dickinson's cavalry. Ellie just stood there and smiled until the shock wore off Tom and Sarah and they rushed forward to hug their grandson and his new wife.

"Careful, Nana," Tucker said as Sarah put her arms around him. She saw him wince and immediately backed away.

"Tucker, are your hurt?" she asked.

""I'm afraid so, Nana. Let's go inside and I'll tell you all about it."

Sarah made a pot of coffee and set it on the table with a basket of biscuits and jam. For the next two hours, Tucker brought his grandparents up-to-date, beginning with the day he left Cracker Landing with Corporal Toby Piggot. He told them that Captain Dickinson's son, Sergeant Charles Dickinson, assigned him sharpshooting duties and he described the skirmishes he and his comrades had been in, including the capture and sinking of the Union gunboat Columbine and the battle outside of Palatka when he was wounded. He also told them about the tragic death of Sergeant Dickinson. They were all aware that Tammy had a crush on the sergeant and they worried how she would take the news.

However, the most emotional part of Tucker's story was about the care he received at the Dancy home, especially from Ellie Westcott and her cousin Lucy. He did not dwell on the seriousness of his wound except to tell them that it prevented him from continuing to serve with his Cavalry Company. Then, he grew more emotional as he told them how he and Ellie fell in love. He said that they decided to marry, even though they had not known each other for very long. However, they could not have a formal wedding because of the Union military activity in the area of the Dancy home. They feared the possibility that Tucker might be captured by Union troops and sent away to be interned at Fort Marion or a more northern prison. Therefore, they sought out the help of a local pastor who married them at the Dancy home in a small, private ceremony.

"Dancy," Tom said pensively. "The name is familiar. Would Colonel Francis Dancy be your uncle?" he asked Ellie. "Yes sir, and James Dancy, my cousin, is the brother of Lucy who is Colonel Dancy's daughter. Do you know him?" she asked.

"I do not know him; however, I know of him," Tom said. "If my recollection is correct, Colonel Dancy is an engineer and he is the man who designed and built the seawall along St.

Augustine's waterfront. However, for a short time he was the mayor of St. Augustine, also."

"That's true," Ellie replied. "And his sympathies are clearly with the Confederacy. That is also one of the reasons he had to flee from our farm. That and the fact that he became a colonel in the Confederate Army."

"Then, your aunt must be Florida Forsythe Reid, the daughter of Robert Reid, Governor of this state when it was still a territory," Sarah said.

"Again, correct, Mrs. Sutter," Ellie responded.

"Mrs. Sutter!" Sarah said in mock shock. "Ellie, dear, you are family now. Why don't you call me the same name Tucker does – Nana. I'd feel much more comfortable if you did!"

Ellie rose from the table, went to Sarah and gave her a hug. "I would be right pleased to do so, Nana," she said as she smiled. "And, may I call you grandpa," she asked Tom.

"Of course!" he said. With that, Ellie was warmly welcomed into the Sutter side of the family.

Lastly, Tucker described the danger of their travel from the Dancy home to the sawmill as they avoided Union patrols. Tucker said that the experience he gained traveling with his cavalry unit using backwoods and swamp trails helped them avoid any serious problems; although they were completely exhausted. That prompted Sarah to insist they get some sleep before dawn arrived. She made up a bed in a spare room of the house and said that they would talk about getting them to Cracker Landing the next morning at breakfast.

The next morning, Tom went to the sawmill early. He told one of the men to ask Captain Bart to come to the Sutter house as soon as he arrived at the mill. Then Tom returned to his house and joined Sarah, Ellie and Tucker for breakfast. Sarah had made fresh cornbread that she served with home-churned butter, fresh fruit and cream. Coffee, however, was another matter.

"Tucker and Ellie, I must apologize for having to serve you Lincoln Coffee," she said. "Ever since the Union blockaded and then occupied the ports of Jacksonville, Fernandina and St. Augustine, real coffee has been hard to come by. We do get some, now and then, however for the most part we have to devise our own. This delicious brew I am pouring for you is made from dried and roasted beet cubes."

"Oh Nana, you cannot imagine what we had to substitute for real coffee when we were on patrol," Tucker said. "How would you like Lincoln Coffee made from cracked, roasted soybeans?" The name Lincoln Coffee was given to just about any substitute coffee southerners had to make when real coffee beans were not available because of the blockades ordered by President Lincoln.

"Uh huh," Tom grunted. "I hear that most Confederate soldiers preferred whiskey to coffee anyway."

"Well, grandpaw, there is something to that," Tucker laughed.

There was a knock on the door and Captain Bart walked in. As soon as he saw Tucker, he threw his cap in the air, shouted hallelujah. He was about to give Tucker a hug but was cut off by Sarah who said, "He's been wounded in the shoulder, Bart."

Captain Bart stopped short, sat down and was filled in on what Tucker had been through. He grinned broadly when he learned Tucker and Ellie were married and he gave her the hug he had planned for Tucker. Then Tom said they needed to get Tucker and Ellie to the Landing as quickly as possible.

"Then, neither Jessie nor Millie know anything about this," Captain Bart said.

"That's right. It will be a wonderful surprise for them," Sarah said.

"However, the Yankees have been arresting any young man who they believe has been fighting for our side," Tom added. "If they do not sign the loyalty oath they throw them in prison. I think, however, that Tucker could be in special danger because he was part of the War Eagle's Company H that did a lot of damage to the Yankees. They might want some revenge."

"Well, we can't have Tucker traveling in those cavalry clothes," Bart opined. "Shouldn't be a problem though. We can round up work clothes from the men in the mill. I have to make a run to the city later this morning, so I can drop Tucker and Ellie off at Cracker Landing. I will bring Ellen because I know she will want to see her favorite nephew. Then, Jessie and Millie can figure out how to handle any unexpected guests from spotting Tucker."

"That's what I was thinking, Bart," Tom agreed. "I am sure Ellen would like to visit Jessie and Millie for a few days and help get these young'uns settled in."

A couple hours later, Captain Bart rounded up his crew who joyfully welcomed back Tucker and delighted in meeting Ellie. They escorted Tucker, Ellie and Ellen aboard the steam barge, tethering Tucker's and Ellie's horses. Captain Bart gave the command to cast off lines and moments later the barge was steaming downriver toward Cracker Landing.

***

The ground was dry, making it easier for the plow to cut through the packed earth and turn the soil. Both Jessie and Joseph were using wheeled single furrow plows to loosen the soil in preparation for planting. Joseph was behind the mule

188

drawn plow while Jessie had hitched the old mare to his plow. This spring, Jessie planned to plow about twenty acres. With a single horse, a man could plow those twenty acres in eight, ten-hour days. A mule was somewhat less effective, so Jessie figured that he and Joseph working together could complete the job in perhaps five days.

The twenty acres they were plowing now was set aside for winter crops that would not be planted until late summer. Their summer crops had been planted a few weeks ago. Jessie was pleased to see that corn, bean, tomato and other summer crops were already growing well in the acreage they plowed late last fall.

"Joseph!" Jessie hollered. "Let's take a break." Wiping the sweat from his face, Joseph, who was two rows west of Jessie, signaled that he agreed. They both unhitched their plow animals and led them to the edge of the fields where a stream ran into the swamp. Letting the animals drink their fill from the stream, Jessie and Joseph splashed their own faces with its cool water and filled their canteens with the tannin-tasting liquid. Then, they sat down to rest in the shade of a live oak tree heavily covered with Spanish Moss.

"Are you OK, Joseph?" Jessie asked, taking a long draw of water from his canteen.

Joseph rested his back against the tree and simply nodded his head.

"I mean, Millie said that lately Anna has seemed unhappy about something. Is there anything you need?"

"No," Joseph replied. Jessie nodded. It was always difficult getting information from Joseph.

"Little Fox and Little flower are growing up real fast," Jessie said, trying to get a conversation going. "You have a fine family, Joseph."

"Umm. Good wife. Good children," Joseph answered.

"But, perhaps something is missing. Yes?" Jessie queried.

"Maybe," Joseph replied. "But not here. Here you and Miz Millie treat us good."

Jessie sensed what the problem might be. Back when Joseph and Anna first came to Cracker Landing, they were practically starving. They were on their way to join the other Seminoles Indians of Chief Billy Bowleg's clan who had escaped the Yankee Army's attempt to capture them in the Okefenokee Swamp. Jessie, Millie and Ellen gave them refuge at Cracker Landing but then changing events prevented Joseph and Anna from continuing their journey. Among other reasons, the Army was forcing all Seminoles and other Indians to relocate from Florida to Oklahoma. Jessie preempted that possibility by registering them as slaves with the Clerk of Court in St. Augustine. However, he believed that Joseph and Anna missed being with the other members of their clan who had likely moved to the "Pahayokee" or "grassy waters," the vast area in the central and southern part of the state settlers called the Everglades.

Jessie was about to ask Joseph if that was what he was thinking about when the shrill whistle of the sawmill steam barge sounded. There were three blasts of the whistle indicating urgency. Jessie and Joseph leaped up, mounted their animals bareback and raced back to the landing - Joseph trailing on the slower mule.

By the time Jessie arrived at the landing, Millie, Anna and Tammy were already there. Jessie dismounted his horse and ran up to the women. Then, stopped short and stared at the barge's two passengers: an attractive young woman accompanied by a tall, lightly bearded young man with a matching mustache. Standing behind the two was Jessie's sister

190

Ellen. It took Jessie only a moment to realize that young man was his son, Tucker. Millie rushed forward as soon as Tucker stepped onto the landing pier and hugged him, as did Tammy. When Tucker winced at the embrace, Millie backed off a little and then noticed the slightly awkward way Tucker was favoring his left arm and shoulder.

"What's wrong, Tucker?" Millie asked, as Jessie stepped forward and carefully embraced his son.

"Nothing to worry about mama. Just got it dinged up a bit a few weeks ago."

The young woman walked up to Tucker and put her arm around his waist. "Meaning that he suffered a minni ball wound to his shoulder, ma'am," she said.

Tucker beamed. "Mama and paw, meet my beautiful wife, Ellie Westcott Beckham!" he said proudly.

Stunned, for a moment, Jessie, Millie and Tammy simply stood wide-eyed. Then tears filled Millie's eyes and she walked up to Ellie and warmly embraced her. She looked at Ellie and brought her over to Jessie, who smiled broadly and also embraced her.

"I guess we have a lot to talk about," Millie declared. She was about to say something else when Stubby, the family hound, came running down the path to the landing trailed by Maggie and three brown and white pups. "What is this all about?" Tucker exclaimed.

Tammy went over to the dogs, who were wagging their tails and jumping on everyone in excitement. She petted each of them, picking up one of the pups and cuddling it in her arms.

"Well, it seems that Stubby did not let his advanced age get in the way of his other interests," Jessie laughed.

"Yeah, and look what happened," Captain Bart said.

"Well, I guess we do have a lot to talk about," Tucker added, as everyone laughed.

"Well then, let's be getting back to the cabin and make some lunch!" Millie suggested. "We can talk about everything over a good meal."

"And, perhaps with a little Cracker Landing Lightning!" Captain Bart added.

There was more laughter and then Millie led the way up the path to the cabin with Tucker at one arm and Ellie at the other. Jessie, Tammy and the others followed close behind. Joseph and Anna ran ahead with the children and were already starting a fire in the outdoor kitchen when everyone arrived. Captain Bart sent Amos to fetch a jug of good Cracker Landing Lightning from the barn. It looked like it was going to be a long and festive lunch. Tucker, however, dreaded the moment of great sadness to come when he would have to tell Tammy that Sergeant Charles Dickinson had been killed in battle.

Chapter Twenty-Four

IT WAS ONE OF THOSE spring days when brilliant white puffy clouds floated in sharp contrast with the deep powder blue of the sky. The temperature was perfect. In the picketed gardens of homes along St. George, Charlotte, and Bay Streets, roses, hibiscus and petunias were in full bloom. Adding to the visual beauty of the day, the air was filled with the delightful odor of orange blossoms from the many small groves that dotted the open areas of the city.

It should have been a time of tranquility and relaxation for the men, women and families who were now milling about the Plaza de la Constitución, as the old parade ground was commonly called. Instead, the crowd seemed to be divided into two major groups. There were those who were shouting celebratory slogans and who were waving banners and the American flag. Others were standing in disbelief – somber and stone-faced. Many of the women in the latter groups wore black and were crying. They had just learned that Confederate General Robert E. Lee had surrendered the Army of Northern Virginia to Union General Ulysses S. Grant at Appomattox Court House, Virginia.

Captain Bart Robinson and his crew were seated on the steps of the old Slave Market, now called the Public Market by the Yankees. Captain Bart, Amos and Shane wore a look of despair on their faces. Henry, the Negro boiler man, made a point of hiding his emotions. Inwardly, however, he was quite pleased.

"I can't believe he shot himself," Shane said. He was referring to Florida Governor John Milton who committed suicide at his Marianna plantation called Sylvania after he learned about Lee's surrender.

"He had everything to be proud about," Captain Bart said. "Tallahassee was the only capital in the Confederacy that was never captured by the Yankees." Amos and Shane nodded in agreement while Henry chose to remain silent, keeping his thoughts to himself.

"I understand he told the Florida Legislature that he did not want to live under the oppression of a lost cause," Captain Bart said. "He was afraid the Yankees would send him to prison if they captured him – which would have been inevitable."

"Look at those people out there," Amos said pointing to the crowds filling the plaza square. "Half the people in town were Yankee sympathizers to begin with or never cared much either way. The rest had no use for the Yankees even though they had to sign a loyalty pledge in order to survive."

"Yep," Captain Bart agreed. "However, there are also those like us who have been lucky enough to live and work outside the city. In many ways, the war has affected us much less than them." Then, in a conspiratorial tone, he added, "And we know what we did for our cause – though in the end it might not have made much of a difference."

Captain Bart was pensive for a minute and then added, "Further, there are our brave young men and women, like Tucker and the Westcott and Dancy girls, who sure as hell helped take the Yankees down a peg."

Amos, Shane and even Henry nodded in agreement. "Well, what now?" Amos asked. "What's to become of all of us?"

"Hell, Lee's surrender does not mean the war is over," Captain Bart retorted. "From what they are saying in the plaza, General Johnston's Army of Tennessee with 90,000 men is still fighting!"

"Damned right!" exclaimed Shane. "Don't forget that Johnston's men are mostly from the Carolinas, Alabama and Florida. Our boys still have a chance to beat the Yankees!"

"Anyway, in my opinion, I don't think much of anything is going to happen to average folk like us," Captain Bart said. "Right now, I think we better get back to the mill and tell them the news."

"What about the Beckhams at Cracker Landing?" Amos asked.

"Yeah, I reckon we best stop there, too. I sure hate to be the one to bear bad news. However, better they find out from us rather than have some smartass Yankee soldiers stop by the landing and tell them."

Later that evening, the sawmill's steam barge made a brief stop at Cracker Landing. Captain Bart was the only one to go ashore. He spoke with Jessie for a few minutes and then resumed the return voyage to the sawmill. Jessie showed little emotion as he walked up the path to the cabin where his family was gathered. There was quiet attentiveness among everyone as he relayed what his brother-in-law had reported to him. Tammy, who had already cried when she learned the news about Sergeant Dickinson, began to cry again, wailing that Charles died in vain. Ellie and Tucker hugged each other while Millie wiped tears from her eyes. Anna, who was helping Millie mend clothes, sat impassively. Then, she got up and went out to find Joseph, who was in the woods tapping pine trees for turpentine.

***

It would be another sixteen months before President Andrew Johnson would formally declare that the insurrection had ended. In the interim, on April 26, 1865, General Johnston surrendered to Union General David Lang at Bennett Place, Durham, North Carolina. Three weeks later, on May 13, 1865, Union General Edward M. McCook was assigned to reestablish Federal control and authority in all parts of Florida. On May 20, 1865, General McCook read President Lincoln's Emancipation Proclamation during a ceremony in Tallahassee. Slavery was officially ended in Florida.

***

When President Lincoln issued the Emancipation Proclamation on January 1, 1863, most of the southern states simply ignored it. After all, eleven southern states had seceded from the Union and formed the Confederate States of America. From their perspective, they were no longer part of the United States of America. Therefore, they were not bound by its laws – most certainly not by a proclamation abolishing slavery. However, at the time the Emancipation Proclamation was made, certain parts of the south were already back under Union control – such as much of northeast Florida from St. Augustine west to the St. Johns River and north to the Georgia border. Within that area, Union troops occupied major cities like Fernandina, Jacksonville and St. Augustine. The interior rural areas were another matter, mostly remaining under the control of Confederate forces.

Nonetheless, within the occupied area slavery was formally abolished. In fact, the Union was able to recruit several thousand former Florida slaves to fight for the northern cause. However, for many slaves who the proclamation freed, there was no place to go and they remained with their former masters performing much the same work as previously. At Cracker Landing, Jessie had to deal with the reality that if they chose, Joseph, Anna and their children could simply walk away and immigrate to Southern Florida where other Seminoles had found refuge. At first, Joseph and Anna chose not to leave the Beckham homestead. Their willingness to remain with the family, and help farm and work the homestead, became even more important when Tucker decided to join Captain Dickinson's cavalry company. However, as was inevitable, one day Joseph and Anna told Jessie and Millie that they had decided to leave Cracker Landing.

All of the women were crying. Jessie, Tucker and Joseph had serious looks on their faces. Little Fox and Little Flower were playing near the barn, chasing chickens. They were oblivious to the somber scene being played out by the adults on the front porch of the cabin.

"I understand why you are leaving," Jessie said to Joseph and Anna. "But, we will miss you very much."

"We will miss all of you, too," Anna replied. "But, we also miss our people." Joseph simply nodded in agreement.

"Well, God be with you," Millie sniffled. There were more hugs among the women and then Anna beckoned to the children. Everyone waved as Joseph, Anna and the children walked toward the woods heading west from the homestead. What few possessions they had were packed on the mule that Jessie gave them in appreciation for helping him work the farm.

Later, on the cabin porch, Ellie asked why the Seminoles did not wait for the next time Captain Bart stopped by the landing so that they could take the barge to St. Augustine. "That would save them a lot of travel, wouldn't it?" Ellie asked.

"Perhaps," Tucker replied. "However, things have changed a lot over the past few years. At one time, we were

197

isolated here at the homestead. It was very difficult to get here except by the sawmill barge or a pole boat. But now, there are a few lumber trails that have been cut through the woods not far to the west of here. Most of those lead to the Old Kings Road between St. Augustine and Jacksonville. Once Joseph and Anna pass beyond the homestead property they will likely pick up one of those trails."

"That's right," Jessie added. "From Old King's Road they will go south and then take the road to Picolata. That is where they will cross the St. John's River. Once on the other side of the river, they will go west to the Ocala and then head south until they reach Seminole country."

"How long will that take, paw?" Tammy asked.

"Not long," Jessie replied. "Two weeks, maybe."

"I sure wish they had waited until after the summer crop season," Millie said. "There is a lot of work to be done out there in the field."

"Yes, there is always work to do on a farm," Ellie said. "At the Dancy farm, with the men gone to war – or killed, we women had to do their work as well as ours. So, don't worry. We will pitch in and do our share to help out."

An hour later, Tammy and Ellie were feeding the pigs when Tammy looked up and saw Joseph at the far end of the crop field walking toward the house. "Paw!" she shouted as she ran up the cabin steps. "Come quick! Joseph is coming back with the mule, but I don't see Anna and there is a man with him!"

Jessie, Tucker and Millie came out onto the porch. Millie stayed on the porch while Jessie and Tucker hurried down the steps and headed toward Joseph to see what the problem was. When they reached him, they saw that the mule the man was leading was not the one Jessie had given to Joseph, who explained what happened.

"Anna and I were walking along one of the lumber trails when we met this man. He said he was looking for Jessie Beckham. I told him I would bring him to you. Anna is waiting for me a couple of miles from here."

With that, Joseph waved goodbye again and walked back along the path leading into the woods. Jessie stared at the man standing in front of him. His gray hair was long and matted and matched the color of his unkempt beard that covered a wrinkled, weathered face. He seemed to be a good five years older than Jessie, but it was difficult to be sure because it was clear the man had lived a hard life. His loose fitting, soiled clothes suggested to Jessie that, like him, he was a man who had worked the land most of his life. Jessie looked into the man's sunken blue eyes and saw a hint of recognition in them. Then, the man spoke, "Jessie?"

"Oh my God!" Jessie exclaimed. "Samuel!"

Cracker Landing

Chapter Twenty-Five

THE NON-STOP BOREDOM of garrison duty at Fort Delles in the Oregon Territory was almost more than Sergeant William Beckham could bear. Fort Delles was an important military post along the Oregon Trail at the point where wagon trains left the trail and continued their journey west on the Columbia River. Protecting The Delles, a French word meaning rapids such as the rapids in the narrow gorge where the fort was located, was vital to settlers traveling the Oregon Trail and to the supply chain for military outposts in the territory. Still, duty at the fort was mostly mundane – except when there were clashes between settlers and roving bands of Yakima or Snake Indians.

William was an eight-year veteran of the Army. He enlisted because he was attracted to the thought of seeing the western part of the country – mainly the vast Oregon Territory that encompassed both Washington and Oregon and even parts of Idaho and Utah. He was not disappointed in the incredible vistas of plains, mountains, desserts and rivers he saw during his tour of duty. However, he was not prepared for the complete boredom of daily life in isolated military posts. The routine at Fort Delles was much the same as at other posts in the western territories:

- **Reveille** or the wakeup call sounded at daybreak.

- **Assembly** or roll call sounded a few minutes later.

- **Sick call** for those who were ill.

- **Mess call** for breakfast sounded at 7:30 a.m.

- **Work details** were sounded after breakfast and the men were detailed from each company for various jobs within and outside the fort.

- **Guard Duty** was on a rotating basis shared by all enlisted men in the company.

- **Retreat** was called at sunset for the lowering of the flag and, perhaps, a parade.

- **Lunch and dinner calls** were timed at the discretion of company commanders and depended on the daily work routine.

William's first enlistment period was for nine months. He renewed it four more times and then war broke out between the north and south. Within months, President Lincoln authorized conscription which meant William had to remain on active duty for the war's duration. During that four-year period, his mother died and he heard from his father, Samuel, less and less frequently. William was worried about his father, especially since he knew that the war was closing in on Florida.

However, the war was over now and William's obligation to the Union Army was completed. During the war he saved half of his $20.00 per month pay so over time, he was able to accumulate almost $500.00. He was also entitled to keep his Union cavalry uniform, although he intended to discard that for civilian clothes as soon as he reached the southern states. He bought a reasonably healthy horse, saddle, saddlebags, horse blanket and other gear for a total of $150.00. An 1860 Henry .44 rim fire repeating rifle cost him an additional $18.00. Then, he bid farewell to his former military comrades, saluted his former commanding officer and rode out of Fort Delles for the last time.

Two months later, a very tired William Beckham arrived at Kansas City, Missouri on a horse that was equally exhausted. Remarkably, the sixty-day trip that took William through Sioux, Shoshone, Kiowa, Crow, Ute and Paiute country, was uneventful. The majority of Indians he encountered were peaceful; either buying supplies or selling goods at military posts or at small settler villages. He felt some discomfort when he traveled through known hostile Indian Territory and spotted armed braves watching him from the top of a ridge or hill. However, he attributed his safe passage through those areas to the fact that he was wearing a cavalry uniform. He suspected that the Indians who saw him had no interest in chancing an encounter with the U.S. Army.

William rested himself and his horse at Kansas City for a few days. He bought a set of denim jeans, jacket and a blue wool shield front shirt that made him look like a wrangler just off the trail. He kept his cavalry boots, however, because they were in excellent condition and fit him comfortably. Also, for the fourth time during his trip, he had a blacksmith re-shoe his horse and he bought an extra set of horseshoes that he carried in the saddlebags that were slung over the stud of the horse's saddle. He still had almost one thousand miles to go before reaching his father's homestead near the 700-acre cotton plantation owned by Charles Bannerman in Leon County, Florida. When he completed his journey, he would have traveled about 2,700 miles over a period of nearly four months.

The terrible effects of the civil war became more apparent to William the farther south he traveled. For example, the city of Memphis, Tennessee had been spared because it surrendered to the Union after the entire Confederate Mississippi River fleet was destroyed by Union gunboats commanded by Flag Officer Charles H. Davis. However, William saw first-hand that the war continued in more subtle ways in the form of racial divide between returning, defeated

Confederate soldiers and the emancipated Negro population. Equally disturbing, the farther south he traveled the more destruction he saw. There were ruined cotton fields, plantations that had been burned and pillaged and a few small towns that had been destroyed by cannon fire and close-in combat. Nonetheless, because most of the civil war battles took place in Virginia, the Carolinas and Georgia, the overall destruction was less than William had feared.

It happened less than one-day's ride to his father's homestead just west of Meriden, Florida. That last night, William made camp outside of Cairo, Georgia on the bank of the Ochlocknee River. The law had broken down in many small towns like Cairo, so William believed he would be safer making overnight camp in secluded places like the off-trail spot he was now preparing to leave. He was excited that by the end of the day he would be home. At the same time, because he had not heard from his father for months, he was apprehensive at what he would find when he reached the homestead.

William had just mounted his horse when he heard the sound of pistol shots and much shouting coming from the trail that ran between Cairo and Meriden. Without warning, a riderless horse broke through the brush, coming to a halt not far from William and his horse. He immediately spotted the blue saddle blanket with gold trim under the McClellan saddle. The letters US in the gold trim of the blanket clearly identified the animal as a U.S. Cavalry horse. William dismounted his own horse and approached the riderless animal that remained stationary as though waiting for a command.

There was no packed bedroll behind the saddle of the horse, indicating that its rider had likely not yet completely broken camp. However, slung over the animal behind the saddle and attached to the saddle stud was a pair of saddlebags with the clearly marked letter US stamped on their flaps. William tethered the horse to a bush and unfastened the flap on the right saddlebag. The bag also had an inner flap that he unfastened, as well. He pulled the inner flap back, looked inside and gasped. The bag was filled with gold coins: $5.00 Liberty gold, $2.50 Liberty Quarter Eagles, $1.00 Indian Head Princess Gold and $20.00 Double Gold Eagles. William estimated that the right side saddlebag probably held several hundred dollars in gold coins. He checked the left saddlebag and found the same – it was filled with gold coins.

William knew this was not payroll money. Union soldiers were paid with paper currency. However, it was the practice of the Army to use gold currency to buy supplies such as foodstuff for the soldiers and hay or oats for the cavalry horses. He speculated that the gold coins in the saddlebags were exactly for that purpose. Mounting his own horse, William took the reins of the cavalry horse and proceeded in the direction the runaway seemed to have come from. He listened carefully for any sounds that might suggest danger. The trail through the woods was quiet. Only the usual forest sounds could be heard: the wind rustling through the pine trees, birds fluttering here and there, the occasional screech of a hawk looking for a meal. Neither of the horses seemed to be spooked, so that was reassuring, as well.

There were two of them, both in full cavalry uniform. One was lying face down, arms stretched forward, as though trying to ease his fall. A revolver was in his right hand. The second trooper was slumped against a tree, eyes wide open as though in disbelief that he had been killed – shot in the stomach. There was no sign of a second cavalry horse. William surmised that either it had spooked and run away or whoever killed the troopers took it with him. He dismounted, took off his wide-brim felt hat and bowed his head muttering a brief prayer for his fallen brother troopers. Then, with his own revolver drawn, he followed a trail of blood a few yards into the woods and found the body of a heavyset man wearing the jacket of a Confederate soldier over a white cotton shirt and black wool trousers. A confederate cap lay next to the body. A well-placed bullet had pierced the man's forehead and had blown off half the back of his head.

He took the saddlebags with the gold coins from the cavalry horse and replaced it with his own saddlebags – the ones containing a spare set of horseshoes. Then, he threw the cavalry saddlebags with the gold on his own horse. Next, he lifted the bodies of the two murdered troopers and laid them over the back of the cavalry horse, securing them in place the best he could. Mounting his own horse again, he led the cavalry horse through the woods until he came upon the main trail from Cairo to Meriden. Slapping the cavalry horse on its haunches, he sent it galloping toward Cairo with its grim cargo. At least they will get a decent burial when someone finds the horse, he hoped. Not having the means to dig even a shallow grave, he left the body of the former Confederate soldier where it lay. Turning south, he spurred his own horse and began the final leg of his journey.

***

Toward the end of the civil war, and for some time afterward, marauding bands of thieves and deserters from the armies of both sides terrorized rural areas in search of food and whatever of value they could steal. In some cases, they simply burned, looted, raped and pillaged in revenge for the losses their side was experiencing. However, in this case, the marauders from Georgia had a special purpose: recover the gold they stole from the union cavalry soldier and his armed escort and reap revenge on the person or persons who absconded with it.

They came three days after William returned home. Both William and his father knew that once the bodies of the troopers were found on the cavalry horse, whoever killed them would also discover that the gold in the saddlebags had been replaced by a set of horseshoes. In a small village like Cairo, someone would speak up and say that the day before the incident, they saw a lone rider pass through town heading south. Meriden was the first town across the Florida-Georgia border. If they rode hard, it should not be difficult to track down that lone rider – and the gold coins. When they reached the outskirts of Meriden, they went from farm to farm asking questions. At most farms, they were shooed away, often with shotguns pointed at them threateningly. But, at one farm, someone mentioned that Samuel Beckham had a son in the army. That was the clue they needed.

Late in the afternoon, five of the ugliest scoundrels you could ever have the misfortune to encounter rode up to Samuel's single-pen farmhouse, carbines resting in front of them on their saddles. Samuel and William both came out of the house and stood on the porch. Samuel was armed with an old musket and William with a loaded revolver in his holster. They were badly outgunned. The five marauders dismounted and approached the two Beckhams. It was over in just a few moments. Samuel managed to get off one shot from his single shot musket before one of the marauders struck him on the head with the butt of his carbine knocking him out. The last thing he remembered was William drawing his revolver.

When Samuel regained consciousness, William was dead and both the house and barn were in flames, as was most of the cotton crop that he had been ready to harvest. He was able to pull a few things out of the house before it was completely destroyed by the fire. However, the barn was already in ashes and what few farm animals he owned were dead or scattered – except for a mule. For Samuel, it was as though the world had ended. There was nothing left to live for – except to bury his son.

The four graves, surrounded by a neatly maintained wood picket fence, were located on a low hill only a hundred yards above the still smoldering ruins of Samuel's homestead.

Three of the graves were marked by a wooden cross he made, himself. Carved on each cross was a name of the deceased and the dates of the person's birth and death. There was very little room on each cross for anything else. Two of the crosses were over twenty years old. They marked the resting places of his parents, Adam and Stella, who died of yellow fever they contracted while visiting him and Rebecca years earlier. The passage of time had left those crosses quite weathered.

Another cross was barely five years old. He knelt before that grave, laid a small bouquet of wild flowers on it, silently telling Rebecca once more how much he had loved her and how much he still missed her. Then Samuel rose and placed a newly carved cross at the head of the grave lying next to Rebecca's – the one containing the body of his son William who he had just finished burying. After securing the cross in the soil, he stood before all four graves and wept.

When he had no more tears to shed, Samuel walked to the cart that had borne the body of his son. He took the reins of the mule hitched to the cart and led the stubborn creature back to the ashes of his cabin and barn. His crops had already been ravaged by half-starving Confederate soldiers from the forces of General John Miller on their way to hold back the Yankees at the battle of Natural Bridge. Now, everything was gone - except the family cemetery with its four graves and the old dry well near the ruins of the cabin.

Samuel dropped the mule's reins and walked to the old well. The frame of the wooden structure was in poor condition suggesting that it had not been used in many years. That was true because some years ago, Samuel dug a new pump well behind the cabin to make it easier for Rebecca to draw water for household chores. He leaned over the edge of the old well, reaching down its side until he felt a rope hooked over an iron spike. He securely grasped the loop of the rope and pulled the heavy object attached to it up and over the well's edge. Tied to the rope were the U.S. Cavalry saddlebags that the marauders had been seeking.

Samuel loaded the saddlebags, a pannier and two pack bags on top of the mule, making sure that the saddlebags were covered from sight. Next, he unhitched the animal from the cart and, with a final glance back at the cemetery, began the long trek east toward Cracker Landing.

***

It was years since Jessie had seen his older brother. If not for the sound of Samuel's voice and the gleam in his eyes, Jessie would not have recognized him. Clearly, life had been hard on his older brother. He conveyed the appearance of a man who was ill and emotionally drained. They stood looking at each other in silence for a moment, neither knowing what to say. Samuel left Cracker Landing while Jessie was still in his teens; so, there really was no emotional bond between the two men. Still, they were brothers.

Jessie stepped forward and approached Samuel, who lowered his head as would a man in defeat. "My God, brother, what has happened to you?" Jessie asked gently.

Samuel was close to breaking down. "They're all gone, Jessie. Everything is gone," he said, his arms hanging loosely at his side as a wave of deep grief overwhelmed him. "First maw and paw and then Rebecca. Now, William. They killed him and burned everything."

Jessie could not stand seeing the suffering on his brother's face. He grasped his brother's shoulders and embraced him compassionately. The pent up emotion Samuel had been holding back broke through and the man sobbed uncontrollably. Tucker, who had been standing next to Jessie took the reins of the mule from Samuels limp hand and led the beast over to the barn. Jessie, his arm around Samuel's shoulders, guided him up to the cabin where the women were tearfully watching the tragic scene that unfolded before them.

Millie decided that the first priority was to prepare a decent meal for Samuel, who, she was certain, had not eaten properly in weeks – probably longer. As she was preparing something for him to eat, she told Tammy and Ellie to heat two big pots of water over the outdoor fire pit. Jessie and Tucker knew what she had in mind so they went into the cabin and brought out the big galvanized metal tub they all used for their weekly baths. Then, after Samuel had eaten his first good meal in a long time, Millie left him in the care of the men who told him to strip and get in the tub which they filled with hot water. Meanwhile, Millie and Ellie, who was pregnant with her and Tucker's first child, searched the cabin for whatever clothing they could find that would fit Samuel's nearly emaciated body. Almost everything they found hung loose on his skeletal frame.

As late evening approached, Samuel had still not offered to discuss how his son William died and who killed him and burned the homestead buildings. He also resisted all of the family's efforts to make him comfortable in the cabin, insisting instead that he sleep in the barn. With Jessie's and Tucker's help, Samuel unpacked the mule and laid his bedroll on fresh hay. Curiously, Samuel took the pair of saddlebags that were under the pannier and mule packs and placed them next to his bedroll. "I will explain everything tomorrow," he said as he curled into the bedroll and quickly drifted off in a deep sleep.

The next morning, Jessie found Samuel in the barn rolling up his bedroll and sorting out the few possessions he brought with him. He decided not to press Samuel for answers, but rather to let him talk about what happened when he was ready. Samuel looked up as Jessie walked into the barn, "I have something to show you," he said to Jessie as he picked up the saddlebags and placed them on a workbench. Each of the dark brown leather pouches measured about fourteen inches by fifteen inches. The leather was well worn but still quite serviceable. They struck Jessie as being unremarkable, except that on the flap of each pouch, the letters US had been stamped, indicating that they were the property of the US Cavalry.

Samuel unfastened the three straps securing the flap of each pouch. He opened the flap of the first pouch and beckoned Jessie to look inside. Jessie leaned over, peered inside and gasped.

Cracker Landing

Chapter Twenty-Six

RACHAEL LEARY JOHNSON DIED at the enviable age of 85. Her husband James preceded her in death by almost ten years. Lucid until her death the past week, Rachael had made it known to her oldest daughter, Beth Rohan and her other two daughters, Laura and Edna, that she wanted to be cremated. She also did not want a big funeral. So, after a private ceremony at the funeral home and a Mass at St. Rita's Roman Catholic Church, Rachael was interred in the Church's columbarium, next to the cremains of her husband.

Laura and Edna lived out of town, Laura in San Diego and Edna in St. Louis. Both daughters returned to their homes immediately after the funeral. Beth and her husband, Tim, lived in Warwick, Rhode Island only a short distance from Bayview, the assisted living center where Rachael lived for the past three years. So, it was left up to Beth to sort through her mother's possessions. At first, it seemed to Beth that it would take only a short time to sort through everything. After all, how much could be stored within the confines of a small studio apartment in an assisted living center? There were a few pieces of jewelry, a closet full of clothes – most not worn in several years – some personal items in Rachael's dresser drawers, a shelf full of books, a TV and a walker with a seat. Of course, there were also a dozen or so framed family photos on the apartment walls. These were all the worldly things a disabled 85-year-old woman needed.

Beth's sisters told her that she was in charge of disposing their mother's possessions. In fact, there was almost nothing that they or the grandchildren wanted. So, Beth worked out a sort of lotto arrangement for the distribution of everything once Rachael's estate was settled. Those would be the only things distributed since Rachael's monetary funds had been depleted some time ago. Most recently, she had been living on Medicaid, supplemented by an allowance provided her monthly by her daughters.

Beth was preparing to leave the apartment when Mrs. Grimaldi, the center's administrator stopped by. She asked Beth what she wanted to do with the box. "What box?" Beth asked. She followed Mrs. Grimaldi to her office where a weathered looking cardboard box sealed with old packing tape sat on a table. "This box," Mrs. Grimaldi said. "Your mother asked us to put it in the resident storage room because she did not have space for it in her apartment."

Somebody had used a magic marker to write the words "Old Photos" on the top of the box. Beth vaguely recalled seeing something like the box in the attic of her mom's house many years ago. She was curious about what might be inside, but not excited. So, she took the box with her and decided to wait until Tim came home from work before opening it. When Tim arrived home, Beth led him into the living room, briefed him on her day at the assisted living center and then showed him the box.

"Well, I can tell you it is pretty old," Tim said. "The packing tape is lifting away from the box in several places indicating the original glue or adhesive has long dried."

"I don't remember seeing it before," Beth replied. "However, I cannot claim to know about everything mom had around the house before she moved to the assisted living center. Let's find out what's inside."

Tim took a penknife out of his pocket and cut the paper tape along the center and side seams of the box. He opened the flaps and looked inside. "Photos," he said, "Just what it said on the top of the box."

Beth peered inside, herself. "Oh, my heavens, look how many of them there are," she said, somewhat dismayed.

After dinner, Beth and Tim began pouring through the contents of the box. There were hundreds of photos; photos of mountains, seashores, weddings, family picnics or gatherings and many, many unrecognizable people who were no doubt long deceased family and friends. There were photos of a river, pier and cabin that must have been taken somewhere in the south because here and there palm trees could be seen. The automobiles in some of the scenes were very old and had to date to the very early 1900s. Then, under one layer of photos, Beth noticed something wrapped in cloth. It seemed to be a packet or small bundle.

The colors in the patterned silk kerchief that was neatly wrapped around the packet were still fresh and vivid. Securing the packet was a single wrap of twine tied in a wide bow. Picking up the small bundle casually, Beth found it to be heavier than she had expected. She called Tim over so he could examine it, also.

"Well, what do we have here?" he said curiously. "Hopefully, it's something that will break the monotony of looking at all these photos."

"It could be deeds or legal papers," Beth replied. "We still haven't found mom's will. That's my fault, actually. I thought mom filed those papers with her attorney a long time ago. But, the paralegal at the attorney's office said she found no record of them."

Beth wrinkled her brow in puzzlement and tugged one end of the twine, allowing it to fall away from the bundle. Then, she carefully unfolded the silk kerchief revealing a cache of letters and what seemed to be a diary or log of some kind – all very old. Both the envelopes and stationery had yellowed over the years. In many cases, the ink had faded to the point that the writing on them was barely legible. Beth sorted through the envelopes, noting sender and addressee names like Dancy, Westcott, Robinson, Beckham, Sutter and Leary; the last surname being that of her maternal grandparents. However, what really caught her attention were the postmarks on the older letters: *Palatka, FL, November 7, 1872, St. Augustine, FL, August 16, 1866, Jacksonville, FL, May 3, 1887* and many other similar dates as far back as one hundred fifty years in the past.

Beth was amazed. She could not wait to read each and every one of them. However, what her eyes were now focused on was a black, leather-bound journal that measured about six inches by nine inches with the word *Memories* on the cover in faded gold foil. As she opened the journal's cover, a small brown envelope fell out. With Tim watching over her shoulders, Beth carefully examined the envelope. It bore the name *Ellie* on its front. Gently lifting the envelope flap, Beth peered inside and inhaled deeply. She turned the envelope upside down and a lock of auburn hair fell out onto the table.

Both Beth and Tim stared at the hair in silence. They had no idea who Ellie was; however, they felt a strange sense of connection with the woman whose hair was on the table in front of them – a woman who had likely died long ago. It was a very emotional moment, especially for Beth, because all of the mementos they had been sorting through had apparently been passed down from her side of the family. Who were these people? Was Ellie one of her ancestors?

Holding the journal in her left hand, Beth began to turn its pages. She flipped past two blank pages and then stopped on the third right hand page. Centered in the page in beautiful handwriting was the name *Ellie Westcott Beckham*. All of the pages in the journal had yellowed with age. However, the ink used to write Ellie's name was still quite clear. Both Beth and Tim were mesmerized. There was another blank page and then the journal began.

Cracker Landing

September 30, 1866

My name is Ellie Westcott Beckham. I am married to the most wonderful man in the world, Tucker Beckham. Tucker is the son of Jessie and Millie Beckham and the brother of Tammy Beckham. The five of us live on the Beckham homestead which is located twelve miles upriver from St. Augustine, Florida and five miles south of the sawmill owned by General John Finnegan that is run by Millie's father, Tom Suller. Tom is married to the former Sarah Perkins. Also working at the Sawmill is Captain Bart Robinson, who is married to my father-in-law's sister, Ellen.

My father was George Westcott and my mother is Amanda Westcott. My father was a cooper and owned a shop on King Street in St. Augustine until he died just before the war. When the Union occupied St. Augustine, they forced my mother and me to leave the city because we would not take an oath of allegiance to the federal government. They confiscated all of our possessions and we were forced to move in with our cousins, the Francis Dancy family near Palatka.

I met Tucker while staying with the Dancy's. Tucker was a member of Captain J. J. Dickinson's Confederate cavalry and was badly wounded at the battle of Nine Mile Swamp. My cousin Lucy and I took care of Tucker after he was brought to the Dancy house by ...

Fascinated by what she was reading, Beth could not put the journal down. She began reading the accounts written by

217

Ellie Beckham aloud so that Tim could follow along with her. In the journal, Ellie recorded a history of the Westcott, Dancy and Beckham families. She wrote about her uncle, John Westcott who became president of the St. John's Railway that once ran between St. Augustine and Tocoi on the St. Johns River. She discussed the hardships that people in northeast Florida, especially Confederate sympathizers, endured during the Civil War: shortages of food and other necessities of life caused first by the Union blockades and then later by the confiscation of crops and farm animals in order to supply the warring troops with food and other material. Most of all, Ellie recorded life at a place called Cracker Landing.

The life on a Cracker homestead in the mid-1800s that Ellie portrayed was difficult at best. In many cases, it was a struggle for survival as homesteaders eked out a bare living working from dawn to dusk. Insects, crop disease, long periods without rain in the early spring, searing hot weather in the summer and the threat of hurricanes in the fall tested them regularly. However, according to Ellie's journal, the Beckhams fared better than many other northeast Florida homesteaders. When the crops were not producing what was needed for their own consumption, much less enough to sell in the public market of St. Augustine, Jessie and Tucker could fall back on their skill producing turpentine. But one day, shortly after the war was over, Jessie's brother Samuel arrived at Cracker Landing and according to Ellie, things began to change.

Beth and Tim shared reading the journal until they finished it shortly after midnight. By then, it seemed that Ellie, Tucker, their children Ethan, Emilie and Mildred and all of the Beckham family, including the Sutters and Robinsons, were not just strangers who lived the better part of one hundred fifty years ago. But rather, if the passage of time could be discounted, they were like close relatives and family friends who you might expect to visit the next day. There were still the letters to read.

However, both Beth and Tim were mentally exhausted and had to put that off to the following morning. For now, their minds were filled with the tales of life at Cracker Landing; a place they had never heard of before and one that very likely might no longer exist.

Beth was unusually quiet and somber as she prepared breakfast the next morning. Tim put his arm around her shoulders and asked what was wrong. "I just don't understand why mom had all of those letters and the journal," she said. "Unless, somehow we are related to those people."

"That's easy enough to find out," Tim replied. "Let's do an ancestry search on the Internet."

It did not take long. Shortly after they finished breakfast, Beth had a printout that caused tears to well in her eyes. She handed the printout to Tim who read it and just shook his head in amazement. "They are all related to you, Beth," he said. "Did you know you were related to the Beckham family?"

Beth was astounded. "No, I had no idea. I did know that my paternal grandparents were, George and Betty Johnson and that their son James married my mother. I also knew that my maternal grandparents were Brian and Linda Leary. I thought Linda was born somewhere in the south. However, she did not want to talk much about her background. Brian was from New York or New Jersey. But, Tim…" Beth said, her eyes moistening with tears again. "Tim, according to the ancestry printout, Ethan Beckham was my grandmother Linda's father. That means that almost certainly, Linda was born at Cracker Landing!"

Beth looked at her husband, her eyes almost pleading for understanding. Then, she collected herself and continued.

"That makes Ethan Beckham my great grandfather! The report says that he and his wife Camilla had three daughters. All of them, including my grandmother Linda, apparently

219

moved away from Cracker Landing after they married. Ethan was the last of the Beckhams."

Beth sniffled a little and continued. "But, Ellie…Tim, Ellie was Ethan's mother and therefore she was my great, great grandmother. I am a direct descendent of this incredible woman who wrote that beautiful journal!" Then emotion overcame her and she began to cry.

They put off going through the letters until the afternoon. Most of them were about family matters: the birth of Tucker and Ellie's children and then their grandchildren, more hardships running the farm, illnesses and the death of Samuel who was killed in an accident while working at the sawmill. One letter referred to an occasion when Jessie and Millie paid off the remaining amount of Captain Bart's loan to the sawmill for the purchase of the steam barge years earlier. That was strange because earlier letters and Ellie's journal often mentioned the financial difficulties they were having. Then, there was a reference to Jessie buying a tract of timberland adjacent to the homestead and contracting to sell the lumber to the sawmill. Where did he get the money to do that?

Finally, they came across a letter Ellie wrote to her mother that explained the mystery of how the Beckhams at Cracker Landing were able to afford some of their later expenditures. In the letter, she confidentially related the entire story about Samuel's son, William, the windfall he came upon when he became the unintended owner of the US Cavalry saddlebags, his tragic death and the reason why Samuel left his homestead and came to Cracker Landing. A few years later, Ellie's mother, Amanda, sent her a note with a cryptic warning saying, "Ellie, don't forget, if you go to the well too often, it might go dry."

Then, there was the last envelope, sealed and obviously containing something heavier than just a few pages of a letter.

220

Beth slit the envelope flap with a letter opener and took out an object wrapped in a cut piece of butcher paper. She unwrapped it and gasped. It was a $2.50 1865 Liberty Quarter Gold Eagle coin in as good condition as the day it must have been minted. Tim and Beth just stared at the coin, not knowing what to say. Finally, Tim hurried over to his computer and began a Google search. A moment later he said, "Beth, that beautiful coin might have been worth only two dollars and fifty cents in 1865, but it is worth a lot more now!"

"You mean its gold value?" Beth asked, holding the coin that weighed a fraction of an ounce.

"No," Tim replied. "According to what I am reading, the coin weighs only .147 of an ounce. At today's prices, its actual melted gold value would be only about $184.00. However, it historical numismatic value is about $4,500.00!"

Beth was shocked with disbelief. "That's fantastic," she said. "That coin must have been among all those in the US Cavalry saddlebags William Beckham stumbled upon on his way back to his father's farm."

"Yes, and remember, those saddlebags were the indirect cause of his death and of his father's ruin," Tim added. "The question is whether that coin is the only one left. It's entirely possible – likely, in fact – that the Beckhams spent all of that money paying off Captain Bart's steam barge debt, buying tracts of timber land and heaven knows what else."

"That brings up an interesting point," Beth said. "What happened to Cracker Landing?"

"Umm, my guess is that Ethan Beckham was not able to continue working the land as he grew older. He and Camilla had only daughters, who, like your grandmother Linda, married and probably moved off the homestead. As time passed and Ethan and Camilla died, the property may have simply gone to

221

ruin. If you drive the country back roads, especially in the south, you can see the ruins of many such houses and barns."

"Well, we now know that one of Ethan and Camilla's daughters was my grandmother, Linda, who married Brian Leary," Beth said. "I am not sure how they met. However, they eventually moved north and lived in Connecticut."

"Where does that leave us?" Tim asked.

"I'm not sure. However, at least now we have a pretty good understanding about the incredible history of my family going back to the Beckhams even before the Civil War. That is absolutely fascinating," Beth said.

"Agreed," Tim said. "Still, I am intrigued by Cracker Landing. I really wonder what happened to the homestead."

"Maybe there is a way we could find out," Beth said. "We have been thinking about moving to a warmer part of the country when we retire. You and I have even talked about buying an older house and fixing it up as a Bed and Breakfast."

"Or, since I love fishing, maybe as a fish camp," Tim said, adding to the possibilities.

"We could consider that, I suppose," Beth replied. "One thing in particular that I find attractive about north Florida is that it is not as crowded as the southern part of the state."

"And it has three seasons, which I like," Tim added. "I'm due for a vacation, so we could drive down there in a couple of weeks or so. Meanwhile, we could see if the county Cracker Landing was in has any records of homesteads in the mid to late 1800s."

Beth smiled broadly and gave Tim a hug. "Sure sounds like a plan to me!"

Chapter Twenty-Seven

Doc CARTER REACHED FOR the crispy hush puppy that was the last vestige of his meal. He took a bite, savored its taste for a moment and then washed it down with the second Corona that Tim Rohan had ordered for him.

"I don't know why I always save the hush puppies for last," he said.

"Everybody has a different way of tackling a meal," Tim replied. "My first bite always seems to be the fries or the slaw. But, I'll be darned, now that you mention it, I guess I usually save the hush puppies for last, also."

The two men laughed and then Doc Carter said, "That was one hell of a story. However, I have a question. Did Ellie's journal record whatever happened to Jessie, Millie and their daughter Tammy?"

"It did. Unfortunately, neither Jessie nor Millie lived more than a few years after Tucker returned to Cracker Landing with Ellie. They died a year apart, both in their fifties. The long hours and hard work required to run a homestead in those days took a terrible toll of people – not to mention the absence of medical care as we know it today. After Jessie and Millie died, Tammy went to live with her aunt Ellen. You will never guess who she married?"

"Who? Don't keep me in suspense," Doc Carter said.

"Amos!" Tim answered.

"You mean Captain Bart's chief deckhand?" Doc Carter said as he slapped the table.

"The very same. He had to be a good fifteen to twenty years older than Tammy," Tim replied. "We are not sure what eventually happened to her or any of those folks. However, we are doing some research and hope we can put together a supplement to Ellie's journal. By the way, do you see that large live oak tree past the barn?"

"I do. What about it?"

"You can't see it from where we are sitting, however, there is a little family cemetery there. That is where Jessie, Millie, Tucker and Ellie are buried. I'll show it to you later."

"I would like that," Doc Carter said. "Well then, apparently Ellie's journal and the letters motivated you and Beth to come down here and set up a fish camp on the old Cracker Landing property."

"It was a little more complicated than that," Tim said. "We did everything we could to locate exactly where Cracker Landing had been. We went to the St. Johns County appraiser's office searching for old homestead records – no luck there. Then we went to the St. Augustine Historical Society's research library."

Tim's thoughts were broken as Jennie came over to the table to see if the men wanted anything else. "How about a piece of mama's key lime pie?" she asked.

"I would love one, except I do not think it would go well with the Corona," Doc Carter said. "How about you, Bubba?" he asked Tim.

224

"Nah, I agree that it would not go well with the beer. Besides, all I need to do is ask Beth to bring a piece home for me tonight!"

"Hmm, on the other hand, I could be persuaded to take a slice to go," Doc Carter said.

Jennie smiled and got up to get Doc Carter a "Take-Home" slice of the pie. Meanwhile, her father continued his story about locating Cracker Landing.

"Adam Beckham bought the Cracker Landing property during the time that Andrew Jackson was offering free or low cost land to induce settlers to come to Florida. It seems the record keeping on those tracts was quite poor at the time. They were further complicated by the process the Territory of Florida was going through as it converted Spanish Land Grants to Territorial and individual ownership."

"However, surely as time passed, the recorded ownership of that tract must have been clarified," Doc Carter suggested.

"Yes and no," Tim answered obliquely. "All that is left of the original homestead is less than ten acres, which is almost entirely encircled by the Deep Creek State Forest. If you look at a map of the forest, you will see one small section in the northeast sector that is private land. That is where we are now."

Tim took another draw from the bottle of Corona Extra and continued.

"With chart in hand, Beth and I rented a pontoon boat from the marina at Camachee Harbor in St. Augustine and took a ride upriver. Pine Island was easily identifiable so we knew that Cracker Landing had been just north and across the river. We would have gone right by it if it had not been for Beth who sighted what seemed to be a tree stump sticking out of the water just offshore. However, that turned out to be part of the old Cracker Landing pier."

"That must have been exciting," Doc Carter said.

"Oh yes. But, not as exciting as when we went ashore and stumbled on the decaying ruins of the main Beckham cabin, the barn and a couple of other structures," Tim explained.

"So, you bought the property."

"Well, the biggest problem, was tracing the land title. It seems that Ethan Beckham died intestate. As time passed without anyone filing a claim for the land, it reverted to the state and eventually became part of a conservation area. Later, all of the original tract, except for these ten acres, was acquired by the state and incorporated into Deep Creek State Forest. Because of conservation use restrictions, the tract was not attractive to local developers. So, we were able to purchase it for only $1,000 per acre. We are restricted from any new development on the property except for restoring previously existing buildings and access thereto. Luckily, there was no restriction on how those buildings could be used."

"Incredible," Doc Carter said. "Was anything left of the original buildings?"

"Not much. We rebuilt and converted the barn as a home for ourselves. Then, we rebuilt the tool shed and, of course, the pier. Lastly, we tackled the original Cracker cabin of the Beckhams which we made into the fish camp store and café."

"That must have been a serious investment."

"Well, I can tell you it took a good part of our retirement savings," Tim said somberly. "However, as you can see, Cracker Landing has turned into a popular spot for fisherman and folks who want a good Cracker meal. In addition, we love living down here."

226

"How about the gold that Samuel brought with him," Doc Carter asked.

"There was not a trace of it, except for the single gold coin," Tim said. "We suppose that the Beckhams spent it all, just like Ellie's journal suggested. But, there was something else. If you have time, I think you would like to see it."

Tim led Doc Carter down the steps of the cabin porch and walked toward the reconstructed tool shed that was next to the outdoor kitchen and the old, covered well.

"We use the outdoor fire pit for barbecues," Tim explained. "I haven't had the cash yet to rebuild the well next to it. But, take a look at this," he said, as he showed Doc Carter a shiny, copper object with coiled tubing leading out from its top into a copper container with a lid on top.

"What the world is that?" Doc Carter questioned.

"That, sir, is the still that the Beckham men used to make what they called Cracker Landing Lightning. Unfortunately, now it is illegal to distill alcohol for personal consumption."

"So, the still is just for show," Doc Carter said.

"I'm afraid so," Tim said as he opened the tool shed door and took a jug off a rack on the wall. "However, I can just imagine Jessie Beckham taking a jug just like this one outside to where his brother-in-law Captain Bart Robinson, the steam barge crew and the men of the family were standing as they watched Millie and the other women prepare a good Cracker dinner."

Tim walked over to the old well and leaned against it. He comically slung the jug over his shoulder as if to take a slug of the fiery liquid that would have been in it. There was a cracking sound as a board he was leaning against split. Tim lost his balance for a minute and dropped the jug into the well.

"Damn!" he shouted. "That was stupid of me. The jug was an antique."

Both men looked down inside the well. "I think you can retrieve it without much trouble, Bubba," Doc Carter said. "It didn't break. Looks like it's sitting in some sand or mud."

Tim quickly got a long, telescopic boat hook from the shed. Meanwhile, Beth heard Tim's exclamation and came down from the cabin with Jennie to join the men.

"What's the problem?" she asked as Tim lowered the boat hook into the well, trying to snag the handle of the jug.

"I stupidly dropped one of the old jugs down there," Tim said. "But, nothing to worry about. It's a dry well."

Beth grabbed Tim's arm tightly. "What did you just say?"

"I said it's a dry well," he replied and then stood up ramrod straight.

"Amanda's letter!" Beth said, running back into the cabin. A moment later, she came running back with both Amanda's letter to Ellie and Ellie's journal. Beth flipped through a couple pages of the letter until she came to the page she was looking for.

"Amanda wanted to give Ellie, Tucker and Tucker's parents a warning to be prudent about something. However, she chose to be circumspect with respect to how she phrased it, probably in case the letter ever fell into someone else's hands."

Beth read from Amanda's letter, "If you go to the well too often, it might go dry." Then she began scouring the journal, finally finding the entry she had been seeking. She looked up at Tim and said, "It's right here, Tim. Samuel and William hid the saddlebags with the gold in a dry well near Samuel's cabin.

They lowered the saddlebags into the well, fastening them on a rope hung from a peg or spike on the well's interior."

"And, this is a dry well," Tim said. "Do you think Samuel and Jessie could have done the same thing here?"

The well was shallow, not more than eight or nine feet deep, easily within the reach of the telescoping boat hook. Tim soon succeeded in latching on to the jug and carefully raised it to the surface where Doc Carter was able to grab it. Then, Tim lowered the boat hook into the well again and began poking around in the sand and mud.

"Wait a minute!" Jennie shouted. She ran back into the cabin and brought out a large LED flashlight. "We need light down there," she said, illuminating the entire inside of the well with the bright beam of the flashlight.

"Look!" Jennie exclaimed. "About a foot down on the right side of the well. It's a spike with something hanging from it – a piece of rope, I think."

Doc Carter reached down and pulled the remnant of rope up. "Sure is a piece of rope," he said. "Tim, poke around on the bottom on this side of the well."

"I feel something solid!" Tim said. He struggled trying to clear the sand off the object with the boat hook and finally something very dark brown or black could be seen. A few minutes later, after much effort with the two men taking turns using the pole to move sand off the object, the vague outline of what seemed to be a saddlebag flap could be seen.

It was much too dangerous for anyone to climb down the well to retrieve it. The walls could cave in on top of the person at any time. However, Doc Carter went to his boat and retrieved a small Danforth anchor with chain and line – the best kind for a mud and sand combination. He skillfully lowered the anchor so that the chain draped over the flap of whatever it was.

Tim helped maneuver the anchor with his boat hook so that when the fluke was pulled, it would slide under the object that more and more looked like leather.

As Doc Carter pulled on the line, Tim used the boat hook to help nudge the fluke forward. Then, the fluke slid right under the object and Doc Carter slowly pulled up the line. An agonizing moment later a pair of mud encased US Cavalry saddlebags could be seen in the LED lights. Everyone held their breath as Doc Carter carefully raised them to the surface.

When the saddlebags reached the top of the well, Tim reached over and helped Doc Carter retrieve them. The men laid the saddlebags on the sandy ground next to the well and together with Beth and Jennie, stared at them for a few minutes, not really knowing what to say. They all realized this was likely the first time that the saddlebags had seen the light of day in over a century.

Beth took off her apron, knelt down and wiped the mud off the saddlebags as best as she could. They were in a remarkable state of preservation, considering where they had rested for so long. Beth was the first to speak.

"Tim, do you think we should chance looking inside?"

"They belonged to your family, Beth. It's your decision."

Beth took a deep breath and unfastened the stiff leather strap securing the flap. She struggled a little, making sure that she did not apply too much force. When the strap fell open, she took another deep breath, looked inside and found an inner flap that she also carefully opened. Finally, she was able to look inside the pouch itself. "It's empty," she said with great disappointment. Everyone exhaled and relaxed.

"Of course it's empty," Tim said. As we surmised, the money was probably all spent even before Ethan and his sisters grew up. The average annual income of a Cracker farmer in the mid to late 1860s was only about $300 to $400. William Beckham estimated that each of the two saddlebags held several hundred dollars. That might have been two or more year's income for someone like Jessie or Tucker – even considering their turpentine business. However, it is easy to see how they would have spent all of that over a period of, say, five or more years."

"Can you imagine how much those gold coins would be worth today?" Beth asked wistfully.

"Well, that's that," Jennie said. "Still, it's neat to have found the saddlebags. They will look great hanging on the wall over the counter."

"How about the other saddlebag?" Doc Carter asked. "You only opened one."

Startled by Doc Carter's observation, the others looked at each other. Almost frantically, Beth turned the saddlebags over to expose the opposite side. Again, she used her apron to wipe the mud away from it. She fumbled with the second set of straps, finally getting them to release. Then she opened both the outer and inner flaps. All four of them peered inside the second saddlebag and gasped.

Photo Album

This is a collection of photos and images in the public domain that illustrate the times, conditions, people and places that would have been familiar to the Beckham family. Some caption character names are fictionalized to conform to the story of Cracker Landing.

Double Pen Cracker Cabin

Cracker Barn

Homestead

Cracker Outdoor Kitchen

Cracker Corral

Diego Swamp

Sawmill

Millie, Jessie, Captain Bart, Amos, Tammy and Tucker

Tucker and Ellie

Seminole Children

243

Captain J. J Dickinson

Capture and Sinking of US Gunboat Columbine

Confederate Soldiers

Fort Marion 1864

(Castillo de San Marcos)

St. Augustine to Tocoi Railroad

St. George Street in St. Augustine 1865

St. Augustine 1858

About the Author

LOUIS E. TAGLIAFERRI is a retired management consultant, publisher, and author. Before his retirement, he was well published as the author of various articles in trade and professional journals and as the author of many business educational works including seven management skills books. Later, he developed an interest in historical fiction. Now, in addition to *Cracker Landing*, Lou is also the author of *Bellaria di Rivergaro*, *The Web Shop*, *The Habsburg Cowboys*, *In Search of Becca and The Virgin of Tears* and *The Timucuan*. Lou lives in Ponte Vedra Beach, Florida with his wife of over 60 years, Judy.

Made in the USA
Middletown, DE
05 September 2020

17217861R00146